A Word from *Voyage of the Basset* Creator James C. Christensen

Years ago, while watching a documentary about Charles Darwin, I realized that something very important had been overlooked on HMS *Beagle*'s historic voyage. I thought to myself, What if someone had sailed in the opposite direction? Not toward science, but toward *imagination*. That was the beginning of *Voyage of the Basset,* a book I wrote and illustrated over a four-year period, and which was published in 1996.

In the book, a professor of mythology and his two daughters, Miranda and Cassandra, board a magical vessel, HMS *Basset.* During their journey, the family visit the court of the fairies, fight loathsome trolls, and discover the secret of the unicorn. Ultimately, they learn how vitally important the imagination is to the human spirit.

Just as the imagination is limitless, so too are the continuing adventures of HMS *Basset!* Some of my favorite authors have signed on to explore new myths and important new truths. The tides of inspiration are with us—shall we board?

Bon voyage!

VOYAGE
OF THE BASSET
THE RAVEN QUEEN

BY TERRI WINDLING
AND
ELLEN STEIBER

Random House 🏠 New York

For Lillian Rhiannon Amos Todd-Jones and
David Taliesin Amos Todd-Jones, good friends of
the faeries, with love
—*T.W.*

For Samantha Jean Lord and Danielle Reed Lord,
who bring magic to my life, with love
—*E.S.*

www.randomhouse.com/kids

Library of Congress Cataloging-in-Publication Data:
Windling, Terri.
The raven queen / Terri Windling and Ellen Steiber.
p. cm. — (Voyage of the basset ; 2)
Summary: Relates the magical adventures of twelve-year-old Gwen and her twin
brother, Devin, on the island of faeries.
ISBN 0-679-89128-5
[1. Adventure and adventurers—Fiction. 2. Fairies—Fiction. 3. Magic—Fiction.
4. Twins—Fiction. 5. Brothers and sisters—Fiction.] I. Title. II. Series.
PZ7.W72437 Rav 1999   [Fic]—dc21   99-42221

Printed in the United States of America   October 1999
10 9 8 7 6 5 4 3 2 1

RANDOM HOUSE and colophon are registered trademarks of Random House, Inc.

Cover illustration by James C. Christensen.

1
A MAGICAL INVITATION

St. Ives, Cornwall, 1874

Devin trudged up the winding cobbled street behind a flock of young Swans. "Flock of Swans" was what his father called the children who lived next door, and indeed, they looked like plump little swans—the boys in spotless white sailor suits and the girls in hot layers of petticoats, dresses, and starched white pinafores. Devin and his twin sister, Gwen, looked like a pair of gypsies beside them, their clothing loose and comfortable, their feet bare and coated with sand. Gwen acted like a gypsy, too, singing all the way up the hill. The Swan children's nanny, leading them home, pinched her lips with disapproval.

At the crest of the hill, Devin turned back to

see his favorite view of the town of St. Ives, with its higgledy-piggledy streets and the blue expanse of the bay beyond them. All winter long, they'd been cooped up in London, but now summer was here at last.

Devin breathed in the fresh salty air, thrilled to be back in Cornwall again. Then Nanny Swan called his name sharply, and he ran to catch up with the others.

"I hate that woman," Gwen complained as her brother reached her side. "Now she thinks she's our nanny, too. And she acts like we're just children! At twelve years old, we're perfectly capable of walking back from the beach on our own. Bother! We went back and forth by ourselves every day last summer."

"But that was before Mrs. Swan complained to Mama about 'children running wild,'" Devin said.

Gwen scowled. "Why does Mama even care what that nosy old biddy thinks?"

"She says we have to get on with the neighbors," Devin explained for the hundredth time, "or else move to another house. And Papa likes it here."

"Of course he does," Gwen said smugly. "We have the best light in St. Ives."

"And so we have to act like other children till Mrs. Swan calms down."

"Hmpf," Gwen replied, tossing her long dark curls. Then she brightened. "At least we're suffering for Art! For the sake of that perfect, beautiful light that Mama and Papa need to paint. But I don't intend to suffer *too* much. Nanny Swan may follow me to every beach in Cornwall if she likes, but if she tries to tell me what to do, I'm not going to listen."

No, I didn't expect you would, Devin thought. Gwen didn't listen to anyone. Except Mama— sometimes. Papa she had wrapped around her little finger.

The flock of Swans met up with a covey of Quayles as they came into Pembrook Crescent, a semicircle of tall white houses with windows looking out on the sea. The Quayle children also were led by a strict nanny in a stiff black dress, starched white apron, and white ruffled cap. The two nannies leaned their heads together as they led their young charges up the road. The sea wind carried their words back to Devin, walking a few yards behind them.

"I see ye got the Thornworth twins to cope with again," said Nanny Quayle.

"And 'tis the last time, ye mark my words," replied Nanny Swan indignantly. "As if I 'aven't got work enough looking after me own little brood. They says to me, 'Here, ye can 'ave two more.' But never again!"

"Wild, by the look of 'em," Nanny Quayle said with disdain. "Disgraceful, it is."

"That girl, Gwen, she's the wild one. There's too much going on in that head. Insisted on a donkey ride, she did, from that man who gives rides on the beach. Then what do ye think she does? Gets up on the donkey's back, waving a wee bit of stick around and shoutin' about King Arthur and such, and then she's took off down the bray! Never knew donkeys moved that fast! Ended in disaster, o' course. She's got a big lump on 'er 'ead now."

"And the boy?"

"Oh, he's no nevermind. Quiet, a bit of a dullard compared to the miss, but at least he's no trouble. He's not like the rest of them Thornworths. Artists, you know. The whole lot of 'em."

"Artists," repeated the other woman sadly, as if it were an illness.

Devin bit his lip. It wasn't the first time he'd heard his family described this way. His father, John Thornworth, was one of the most sought-after painters in England—his work hung in London galleries alongside the paintings of Rossetti, Millais, and Burne-Jones. Devin's mother, May, was an artist, too, painting portraits for rich and fashionable ladies. And yet the Thornworth family was viewed with deep suspicion in Pembrook Crescent. Artists could be famous in London, but that didn't make them respectable here—not, at least, to the families of bankers and lawyers who were their neighbors. To bankers' wives, it was little short of scandalous that May Thornworth worked—that she had her own career and her own studio, alongside her husband's. Devin's elder sisters, Vivien and Elaine, were painters, too, studying with Whistler this summer. That was another scandal—young women studying art as if they were young men.

And then there was the matter of clothes. Mama, Papa, and their painter friends were part of the Pre-Raphaelite movement. That meant that while everyone else wore uncomfortable layers of clothes buttoned neck to ankle, Mama wore flowing dresses of velvet or silk like a fairy-tale heroine, her thick auburn hair worn loose and rippling over her shoulders. All of her daughters dressed the same way—even Gwen (when she wasn't decked out as a pirate, a faery, or a Knight of the Round Table).

Devin himself never wore short pants and stockings like other boys—he wore long trousers, just like a grown man, with a collarless shirt or a painter's smock. But his smocks, unlike Papa's and Mama's, were never stained with drips of paint. Devin couldn't paint. He couldn't draw. In fact, it seemed increasingly obvious to everyone that the son of the great

John Thornworth had no real artistic ability whatsoever.

As they reached the end of Pembrook Crescent, Nanny Swan and the little Swans climbed the stairs to Sea View House while the twins went on to their own house, Camelot, at the far end of the row. Devin paused on Camelot's steps, watching the Swan children disappear with a feeling that was almost envy. He didn't want to be one of them, of course, marched around town by their horrible nanny. But Sea View House was clean and quiet. The furniture was comfortable—unlike their own Pre-Raphaelite beds and chairs, beautiful but hard as boards. The Swan children would have a good, plain dinner awaiting them in the day nursery. In his house, there might be a feast of exotic, extravagant, and (to Devin) inedible food—or else there might be nothing at all if Mama, caught up in painting or poetry, forgot to speak to Cook.

He sighed as he turned the heavy glass doorknob, braced for the usual chaos. Inside, someone was banging piano scales, Vivien's dogs were barking, and Elaine's demented parrot was shrieking about the Lady of Shalott. Gwen pushed past him and ran down the hall, her bare feet thudding noisily, the hem of her long linen shift trailing wet sand.

"Mama!" she yelled.

"In here, princess," Mama called out from the back of the house. Devin followed Gwen and found their mother in the dining room, talking to the cook. Dressed in a long blue painter's smock, her auburn hair pinned back on her neck, Mama looked like those romantic, dreamy women in Rossetti paintings. As Gwen stood beside her, Devin was struck by how much the two resembled each other. His sister had that same thick hair, milky skin, and velvet brown eyes.

May Thornworth turned her eyes on her quiet son and breathed a sigh of relief. "Here's my Dev. My practical boy. He'll sort everything out, Mrs. Pedwyn. I must get back to my sitters now. They've come to see their finished portrait."

She brushed her son's cheek with her lips as she passed. Devin felt a warm glow within. He might not be an artist himself, but at least he knew how to look after them. *Someone* had to look after his family. They all lived in a world of dreams—Mama, Papa, Vivien, Elaine, and especially Gwenevere. They lived in paintings and poetry and tales of King Arthur's magical court. But here in the real world, someone had to organize things and keep the household running.

"Mama, wait!" Gwen followed her mother. "I have to tell you about our adventure! Well, it was *my* adventure, really. Devin is just so useless sometimes, and he has *no* imagination. He was supposed to be Sir Percival, and I was the tragic Sir Lancelot, and I rode a donkey as my steed and set off for Chapel Perilous and..."

Gwen's voice faded down the hallway, along with her mother's soft laughter.

Cook was flustered and worried, as usual. Even though she'd spent many years with the Thornworths, she still wasn't quite used to their ways. "Oh, my weak heart," she moaned, sitting down, one hand pressed against her chest. "Master Devin, whatever shall we do? No one has paid the grocer's bill yet, his boy has refused to deliver this week, and I've but a meager dinner put on, made up of what we had in the house. And now Her Ladyship says she's invited her sitters to come to dinner!"

"Tell me what you need," said Devin.

"Oh, there's no time left to make nothing else," Cook began, working herself into a state. "And them two ladies, they look awfully grand. And us with no food in the house!"

"Now, now," said Devin soothingly, "I'll go and fetch my father's purse. You can send the coal boy down to that fancy shop on Pilchard Street. They'll make up a big picnic basket for us. We'll spread a blanket on the lawn and pretend we're on holiday."

"I can't feed ladies on the lawn! Them in their

fancy good clothes and all!"

"Of course you can. Fine ladies get tired of eating off silver and china, you know. They'll think it's a grand adventure—and Mama and Papa will make it seem like one."

"You're right about that, Master Devin," said Cook. She smiled suddenly. "You're a dependable lad, I'll say that for you. Not like the rest of your family at all."

No, he wasn't like the rest, which was a thing that troubled him. The others were wonderful, fascinating, and outrageously talented. *And I'm just dependable,* he thought glumly as he left the room.

The boy walked down a long hallway (brightened by rose-covered wallpaper made by Papa's great friend Mr. Morris), through a small conservatory, and out into a sunny garden. A path of slate shingles wound through hedges, flower beds, and old apple trees. At the very back was the big stone barn that Papa had christened Avalon. It was fitted out with a row of north-facing windows, and doors at either end—one leading into Papa's studio, the other into Mama's.

Devin knocked on the left-hand door. It was opened by the skinny little man who worked as Papa's studio assistant, preparing paints, cleaning out brushes, and scaring away visitors who might distract the great artist at work. Papa was standing on a high platform that allowed him to reach the top of a painting nearly as tall as Avalon's roof. It pictured the wizard Merlin trapped in a tree by a faery sorceress—a scene from Papa's favorite poem by Mr. Tennyson. A gypsy man was posing for Papa, dressed like Merlin in a long wizard's cloak. These models were another reason the neighbors didn't approve of his parents. For reasons the boy never understood, models were deemed to be scandalous, too. Devin liked the gypsy man, who'd posed as King Arthur the year before and the Fisher King the year before that. He often told Devin spine-tingling stories about the gypsy life.

"Your father is working," the studio assistant warned, but Devin ignored him.

"Cook needs grocery money," he yelled up to Papa.

"You know where it is," the painter yelled back, never turning, never stopping his brushstrokes. Merlin winked at the boy.

Devin plucked the purse from a pocket of his father's coat, hanging by the door. "Mum has invited her sitters to dinner," the boy called up.

His father grunted in reply. Devin didn't mind. John Thornworth was deeply absorbed and would stay that way until dusk. When the light finally failed, he'd blink, return to himself, and remember his family.

Devin weighed the purse speculatively as he left the studio; then he stopped on the narrow porch outside and opened it. As he counted coins, he could heard the sound of voices. One of them was Gwenevere's. It came from the other end of the barn, where a low bench sat in an oak tree's shade. He spied two elegant ladies there, with Gwenevere perched at their feet. He recognized the ladies. They were Mama's sitters—known as the Aisling sisters, although they both had different married names. Mama had painted a very nice portrait of them, and they'd come to pick it up. It was meant to be a gift for their father, who lived in a foreign land.

Devin wondered what Gwen was saying to them, and why she was looking flushed and excited. Never mind. It would soon be dinnertime, and Cook would be having heart palpitations. Devin started up the path to the house—and spied a flash of light through the trees. It came from the spot where Gwen was sitting. In fact, it came from Gwen herself. She was holding something that flashed and sparkled and pulsed in her hand, like a star.

Devin started toward his twin. He was curious, drawn by the light. "You see, Miranda?" said one of the ladies, exultant. "I felt it! I knew it all along!"

"Yes, yes, you were right, Cassandra. But you needn't tell the whole neighborhood!" The elder sister turned to Gwen. "You are indeed the one we have come to find, Gwenevere. There can be no doubt of it now. The necklace you hold is from the Lands of Legend. It tells us you are the one."

"The one?" Gwen breathed.

"The one who will sail on the *Basset*," Cassandra answered. "The one with imagination, and courage, and a deep desire for magic."

Miranda said, "The ship has been here since dawn, waiting for you in the harbor. It sails tonight. Our portrait is finished and ready to go, if you will please take it. The painting is for our father—but we're not sure where he may be found these days. Deliver it to Titania, the Faery Queen, and she'll pass it on."

Devin stopped in his tracks. The Faery Queen? Oh, bother. It was just some play they were acting out—some silly pretend thing. Gwen handed the necklace back to the woman called Cassandra. It wasn't sparkling now. Devin shook his head. It had been a trick of the light. He turned back to the house.

"Do you like adventures, child?" he heard one of the women ask Gwen eagerly.

"Oh, yes," said Gwen.

"Oh, no," muttered Devin. She'd be impossible

tonight. All wound up in this game of theirs, wanting him to play some part. She'd want him to wear some wretched costume, and then she'd call him useless again. Maybe he could go off and hide with a book as soon as dinner was done. But he knew he'd probably stick around to keep an eye on his headstrong twin. Just in case, in the name of adventure, she went and did something daft.

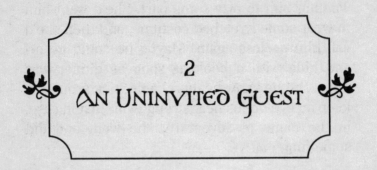

2
AN UNINVITED GUEST

Gwen raced up the staircase to the second floor, down a long, dark corridor, and into the room she shared with her sisters—a lovely chaotic mess of books, paints, clothes, seashells, and half-drunk cups of tea. Fortunately, her sisters were staying in London tonight. Gwen flung herself down on her beautiful bed, which Papa had painted with maidens and flowers. She'd just spent an endless evening, waiting until everyone else in the household was asleep so her journey could begin.

Cassandra's necklace pulsed and sparkled for me, she thought happily. *I've been chosen to sail on the* Basset. *I am going to deliver Mama's portrait of the Aisling sisters to the Queen of Faery and have the most enchanting time!*

It didn't surprise Gwen in the least that she'd

been chosen to sail on the *Basset*. She'd always known that she was destined for fantastic, magical adventures. The only real surprise was that it had taken so long for this to happen.

I must be sure to pay very close attention, Gwen thought. *For I shall have to tell Dev and Vivien and Elaine all about my adventures.*

Better yet, she'd take her sketchbook and charcoals, so she could draw the faery court. And her watercolors and brushes and colored chalks, as well. Gwen jumped up, went over to her desk, and opened the tin box of art supplies that she kept there in case she woke in the middle of the night with what Papa called "raging inspiration." This had never actually happened to Gwen, but her father said it happened to him all the time, so she felt it was best to be prepared.

She carefully chose the art supplies she would need for her journey. Then she rolled up Mama's painting of the Aisling sisters and tied it with a green hair ribbon. (Cassandra had taken the canvas off its heavy wooden stretcher, so that it would be easier to carry.) Gwen rummaged through the big wardrobe in her room and dragged out the largest of her valises. She had quite a few things that she needed to pack.

First she threw in her long midnight blue velvet cloak. After all, one couldn't go on an ocean voyage without a cloak to billow romantically in the wind. Then she chose a dress of deep red velvet with golden flowers embroidered on the yoke. She wanted to wear her absolutely most magical dress when she met the faeries. She added her favorite cambric nightgown, a petticoat, a pair of boots (in case her feet got wet on the boat—she'd heard that boat decks could get quite soggy), her kid-leather gloves, her best hat, a hairbrush and ribbons, and her mackintosh in case there was a storm at sea.

But when she tried to fasten the latches on the valise, she found that it wouldn't close. The mound of clothing and art supplies was spilling out the sides onto her bed.

"Oh, bother!" Gwen muttered. She'd have to leave something home...unless Devin organized it for her. Packed neat and tidy, it just might all fit. Devin always organized the family packing when they left London each summer. Everyone left the things he or she wanted to bring to St. Ives piled on his or her bed, and then Dev saw to it that everything was neatly folded and fit into their assorted suitcases and trunks. It wasn't fair, though, to ask Dev to pack for her this time—not when he wasn't coming along. She knew it would hurt his feelings when he found out that she'd been invited to sail on the *Basset* and he hadn't.

Hands on hips, Gwen glared at her valise. Finally, she took out the mack and the boots. Her art supplies, though, were essential. She was sure she would be called upon to create beautiful art for the faery court. Gwen tried to close the valise again and was pleased when it shut quite easily.

That it was it, then! She took one last glance around the room. Her eyes lingered on the old tapestry above her bed. Gwen had always thought it utterly magical. The tapestry showed a lush green wood. In the center of the wood, a young woman in a blue silk dress sat beneath a rowan tree with silver leaves. The young woman had long dark wavy hair, very much like Gwen's. (Gwen liked to think they resembled each other.) A white horse grazed calmly beside the young woman. A raven—with its head cocked and right eye shut—perched on her shoulder. A slender mink slept curled in her lap. (Actually, there was some debate in the Thornworth house about the "mink." Her mother called it a ferret, her father thought it was a weasel, and Dev referred to it as "that sleepy little rodent.") Whatever it was, the young woman stroked it gently with one hand. In her other hand, she held a golden sphere.

The tapestry had been hung in the room when Gwen was four and had been confined to bed with a high fever. She remembered lying in bed, staring at the tapestry, and calling on its three animals. Since then, she'd always secretly believed that they were the ones who cured her fever. She liked to think of them as her animal helpers, like the ones in folktales.

Now Gwen addressed them once more. "Raven, horse, mink," she whispered, "take good care of everyone here while I'm gone."

She picked up the valise with one hand and the rolled-up painting with the other, and tiptoed down the hallway. One of the hall gas lamps was lit, but she couldn't see any lights beneath the bedroom doors. Everyone in the household was asleep. Nevertheless, she walked as quietly as she could past her parents' room. It wasn't that she thought Mama or Papa would object to her sailing on the *Basset*. They loved the old tales and Tennyson's poems about knights and maidens and faeries and quests—so how could they object if Gwen had been called on a quest of her own? Still, with Mrs. Swan next door telling them that twelve-year-olds should be treated like babies, perhaps it was best to have her adventure first and tell them about it later.

Gwen breathed a little easier once she reached the bottom of the stairs. She let herself out the front door and stepped into the night. But it was a very dark, fogbound night and there weren't any stars out. She hadn't gotten more than four steps from the porch when she realized that if she didn't carry some kind of light, she would end up pitching headlong down the steep cobbled road. So with a sigh (was this any way to begin a grand adventure?), she returned to the house for a lantern, lit it, and then started out again. This time she carried the valise with her right hand and the lantern with her left, the painting tucked beneath her right arm.

The flame inside the glass lantern flickered with every step, casting shadows around her. It suddenly felt odd and a bit lonely to be setting off through the dark streets of St. Ives with no one to hug her good-bye or wish her safe journey.

Slowly, Gwen made her way through the narrow, winding streets. The town was silent. The slate-shingled houses were dark, and the little shops all shuttered. The only sound came from the harbor—the steady lap of waves against the shore—and even that sound was muted by the fog.

Gwen's valise got heavier with each step. She kept having to set it down and rest. The waterfront seemed miles away, and it suddenly occurred to Gwen that she might miss the sailing of the ship. The Aisling sisters had not been very specific about when it would leave. Miranda said only that the *Basset* sailed tonight. Gwen dearly hoped that it hadn't left yet, but the fog was so thick that she couldn't see the lights of the docks or the boats.

She was halfway down the hill when she heard it—another set of footsteps. Someone else was out here, behind her. Gwen spun around and held the lantern high. But she saw only glistening droplets of mist.

I must be imagining things, Gwen decided, and set off again. But a few moments later, she heard the footsteps again. This time she was very sure she was not imagining them. Someone was following her.

Gwen felt her chest constrict with fear. She did the only thing she could think of. She held the valise as high as she could and began running toward the harbor.

The cobblestones beneath her feet were slick from the mists. Gwen hadn't run more than five yards when her right foot slipped, and she, the lantern, and the valise all tumbled to the ground. The lantern's glass broke, and the candle's flame vanished.

Gwen clamped her hand over her mouth to keep from crying out. And then she heard a familiar voice.

"Gwen, are you all right?"

It was Devin. Gwen's racing heart slowed to a more regular beat. She got to her feet, sputtering with anger. "How dare you follow me like this? You nearly scared me out of my skin!"

She heard the sound of a match being struck.

Seconds later, Devin lit a lantern of his own. He looked pale and frightened in its flickering light. "What are you doing?" he asked, taking in her valise and the smashed lantern. "Where are you going?"

Gwen fought down a surge of impatience. "I can't really explain now," she said, "but I'm perfectly fine, and there's nothing to worry about." She brushed herself off and grabbed the valise.

"I think you forgot this," Devin said. He bent down and handed her Mama's painting.

"Thank you," Gwen said stiffly, then started down the hill again. Devin fell into step beside her.

"Dev, you cannot follow me!" Gwen told him.

"I am, though," he replied mildly.

Gwen had to set the valise down again. Devin rolled his eyes and picked it up. Although they were exactly the same height, his arms were much stronger than hers—which annoyed Gwen no end. "I didn't ask for your help!" she snapped.

"Well, you weren't doing a very good job of carrying it yourself," Devin pointed out in a reasonable tone. He glanced down at the valise. "What did you pack in here—baby elephants?"

The last thing Gwen wanted was for Dev to walk her to the *Basset* and then be told he couldn't come aboard. She already felt bad for having said that afternoon that he had no imagination. She didn't want him to be turned away from a wonderful adventure for the same reason.

"Devin, please go back home," she tried again.

But Devin kept walking toward the waterfront. "Not until you tell me where you're going."

Gwen would have screamed with frustration if she hadn't been sure it would wake all of St. Ives. Her brother could be so stubborn!

She hurried after him. "I'll tell you everything as soon as I get back," she promised.

"Where you're going—it's connected to the women who sat for Mama, isn't it?" Devin asked.

Gwen nodded. They were at the bottom of the hill now. The salt tang in the air was sharp, and she could hear the water swelling against the piers. The docks were dark, except one in the distance that was dimly lit. Gwen's pace quickened as she saw the outline of a small ship in its light.

"You're going off on this *Basset* boat?" Devin persisted.

"You were eavesdropping!" she said accusingly.

"I overheard you by accident," he protested. "But Gwen, you're not serious about this?"

"Of course I am. Do you think I snuck out in the middle of the night for exercise?" Gwen saw a flicker of hurt in Devin's eyes and instantly regretted her sharp words.

"Look," she said more gently. "This is terribly important to me. All my life I've dreamed of meeting faeries. I've painted them, and drawn them, and left milk out for them at night like Cook's old granny used to do. Now at last I have a chance to see them! To actually enter their realm and meet Titania and Oberon and dance with them in a faery ring beneath the moon!"

"Good luck finding the moon if Faery is as foggy as Cornwall," Devin muttered.

"It won't be," Gwen assured him. "Faery is going to be beautiful and dazzling and perfectly gorgeous."

Dev rocked back on his heels. "What about Mama and Papa?"

"What about them?" Gwen countered. "Papa's been painting magical pictures all his life. You know he'd be thrilled for me! And Mama, too."

"Then why didn't you tell them you were going?"

Gwen shrugged. "It…seemed easier this way. Besides, I'm just going to deliver this painting and sail right back. With Papa's exhibition coming up, they won't even notice I'm gone."

"I'll notice," Devin said quietly.

Somewhere across the water, a foghorn called. Gwen felt as though it were summoning her to the *Basset*. Besides, she'd wasted enough time with this pointless argument. "Dev, *please* go on home. I'll be back soon, I promise."

"It's not a good idea," her brother told her. "This entire midnight journey of yours…It's not practical."

"But it *is* fabulously romantic," Gwen told him. "Besides, you can't stop me!" With that, she yanked the valise from Devin's hand and hurried toward the boat.

Gwen pushed herself to a run, the soles of her shoes slapping against the wet cobblestones, the valise bumping against her legs. She ran past the docks where the fishing boats came in and the pier where the passenger ferries to Ireland docked. She ran until she reached a narrow, deserted dock—where the oddest, most beautiful sailing ship she'd ever seen was moored. It was a small ship with three masts and an elaborately carved bow. Below the deck, three arched windows were lit. Gwen was sure she could see the sparkle of chandeliers inside.

A wooden gangplank stretched from the ship down to the dock. Hesitantly, Gwen stepped onto the plank.

"Hullo!" she called loudly. "Is anyone there?"

A short bearded man dressed in a silk coat and a gold vest peered down at her from the deck. "Good evening," he said. "Are you, by any chance, Miss Gwenevere Thornworth?"

"I am," Gwen said. "But please call me Gwenevere."

The little man bowed to her. "I am Archimedes, helmsman for HMS *Basset*. Welcome aboard, Miss Gwenevere."

Gwen was halfway up the gangplank when a troop of even tinier men—or were they boys?—scurried toward her. They all wore identical red jackets, pinstriped pants, spats, and absurdly tall black stovepipe hats. They were so quick that Gwen couldn't follow their movements. In a blink of an eye, they'd taken the valise from her. Turning it on its side, six of them hoisted it overhead and carried it on board.

"Thank you," Gwen said, somewhat startled.

She stepped onto the deck and glanced around. With a jolt of surprise, she realized that she was the tallest person on board. The entire crew of the *Basset* was made up of dwarves and the little beings in the stovepipe hats.

A distinguished-looking dwarf with reddish hair and long sideburns that met in a beard stepped forward. "I am Captain Malachi," he explained. "This is my crew." He nodded to five equally distinguished-looking dwarves standing behind him. "And these"—he gestured to a group of the tiny men who were now bouncing up and down on Gwen's valise—"are the gremlins. They help out, too, in their way."

"When they're not causing chaos," muttered one of the dwarves.

"You arrived at a most fortunate moment, Miss Thornworth," Captain Malachi went on. "The tides of inspiration are in, and we are ready to set sail."

"To Titania and Oberon's island?" Gwen asked. She had to be sure. "I have a very important painting to give them for Professor Aisling."

The captain's face wrinkled with a smile. "Professor Aisling is a dear friend," he said. "It will be our pleasure to take you to the island of the faeries so that you may deliver your painting. Bosun Eli, weigh anchor! Helmsman Archimedes, hard alee! Seaman Augustus, raise the banner!"

The dwarves and the gremlins immediately became very busy. Ropes were loosed and sails were raised. Gwen looked up as a beautiful turquoise silk banner snapped open. Words had been embroidered on it, but Gwen didn't recognize them.

"'Credendo Vides'?" she read aloud.

"By believing, one sees," explained a dwarf with spectacles and a long white beard. He gave Gwen a warm smile. "I am Sebastian, the first mate. As soon as we're out of the harbor, I'll be happy to give you a tour of the ship."

"Would it be all right if I came along, too?" asked a hesitant voice.

Gwen spun toward the dock in disbelief. Devin stood at the top of the gangplank, looking awkward and uncertain.

"No!" she said at once. "Miranda's locket glowed for me, not you. *I* was the one chosen for this adventure. You don't think it's *practical*," she reminded him.

"There's nothing wrong with being practical," Sebastian said thoughtfully. "Dwarves are actually quite practical. While the gremlins are more...spontaneous." He squinted through his spectacles at the boy on the gangplank. "If you don't mind my asking," he said in a very polite voice, "who are you?"

"Devin Thornworth," the boy answered.

"My twin," Gwen explained. "Well, not really. He's more my younger brother. I'm older by thirteen minutes."

Sebastian took off his spectacles and polished the lenses with his handkerchief. "I believe this is a matter for Captain Malachi," he said at last. "He's still cross with me for inviting that badly behaved Hepzibah child on board. Wait there, please—I'll be right back."

Dev looked so thoroughly miserable, Gwen almost regretted the things she'd said. But she didn't want her brother, with all of his terribly practical concerns, ruining the most magical adventure of her life.

Moments later, Captain Malachi walked toward them, his hands clasped behind his back. He fixed a stern gaze on Devin. "Young man, if you would be so good as to come up on deck for a moment—"

Devin swallowed hard and stepped onto the *Basset*.

"Now," said the captain, "what seems to be the problem?"

Gwen was determined to have the first word. "This is my *younger* brother, Devin," she began, "who, against my wishes, followed me down here—"

"Only because I was worried about you," Devin broke in. "I thought you were off on another one of your made-up adventures."

"I assure you, the *Basset* is quite real," the captain said.

Dev's cheeks flared red in the lantern light. "I see that now," he said. "I—I didn't mean any harm."

"No harm taken," the captain assured him.

Something about the captain's cordial tone worried Gwen. "You're not going to let him stay on board, are you?" she asked.

"That question has already been settled," the captain replied. "The gremlins have drawn up the gangplank and set sail. You are now both guests of HMS *Basset*."

"Oh. Thank you…I think," Devin said as the captain called another order to the crew and strode away. Dev gave his sister a mystified shrug. "Looks like we're mates, Gwen."

"Gwenevere," she told him. "On this adventure, I'd prefer to be addressed as *Gwenevere.* And I can't *believe* you did this!"

"Neither can I," Dev admitted. "All I wanted to do was see what you were up to—not wind up on an ocean voyage."

Gwen swayed a little as the *Basset* moved out onto the water. "Well, you did. And it's my ocean voyage and my magical adventure, and now I'm stuck with my younger brother!"

"Your ocean voyage?" Devin said. "You sound as though you bought the ship. And what is all this *younger* brother stuff? When did we stop being twins?"

"When you started following me around like a nursemaid!" Gwen snapped.

But Devin, it seemed, had forgotten their argument. He was watching one of the gremlins scale the rigging to the crow's nest. "Look at that!" he said. "That little fellow's an extraordinary climber!"

"Set the *wuntarlabe* for the Isle of Myth!" Captain Malachi's voice boomed out.

"What's a voonterlob?" Devin asked, looking around.

A dwarf with a blond beard trimmed to a neat point appeared at his side. "I am Seaman Augustus," he said, "and the *wuntarlabe* is the instrument that allows us to navigate the seas of the imagination. Would you two like to observe it?"

"Absolutely," Devin said. Gwen wasn't interested in navigational instruments, but it seemed rude to refuse. So she followed her brother and Seaman Augustus to the forecastle, where the rest of the dwarves were gathered around a very odd instrument. It was made of silver and copper with gold bells and brass buttons. Even a few precious stones sparkled here and there.

"Amazing," Devin said, leaning in for a better look.

"Is it?" Gwen asked. She was feeling more and more cranky by the second. *Her* magical journey was not supposed to begin with admiring an odd little machine.

"Well, yes," her brother said. "See, it's got all these gears and arrows and scales and wheels on it. It looks like a combination compass-weather-vane-barometer-measuring device."

"Very good, Master Devin," said Archimedes. "That is, more or less, what it is." He stepped up to the *wuntarlabe* and carefully set several of the dials and gauges. Then he stepped back, and one of the little gremlins popped forward. The gremlin's hat was pulled so far down over his eyes that

Gwen wondered if he could see at all. But he climbed up onto a stool, pressed two brass buttons, then whirled one of the silver wheels.

Gwen watched in amazement as the *wuntarlabe* whistled and popped, jingled and whirred. Sparks flew from the gears, the jewels flashed, and all of the arrows revolved madly. At last with a THWOCK and a WHOOSH and a SPROING! the *wuntarlabe* stopped vibrating, and the largest arrow of all pointed THAT WAY!

"Our course is set," Captain Malachi declared.

"I don't understand," Gwen said crossly. "You've sailed to the faery island before, which means you must know where it is. So why do you need this vunter-whatever?"

"Do you really think the island of faeries remains in one place?" Archimedes asked kindly. "There are very few fixed points in the realms of the imagination."

"That actually sort of makes sense," Dev said. He and Archimedes then launched into a discussion of latitudes and longitudes, which Gwen found extremely boring.

Fortunately, Sebastian found her then. "Miss Gwenevere," he said, "may I show you to your quarters?"

"That would be lovely," she replied, and followed him belowdecks. Gwen's spirits rose as she found herself in a grand hall lit by a crystal chandelier. In fact, the hall seemed much larger than the deck above. Gwen couldn't imagine how it fit on the same small ship.

"Your room," Sebastian said, opening a door. Gwen stepped inside and gasped with delight. It was a room fit for a princess—with a canopy bed, a golden mirror, and a dressing table made of polished rose quartz.

Her valise and the painting were lying on the bed. She opened the suitcase, took out her red velvet dress, and carried it to the wardrobe to hang it up. But when she opened the wardrobe, she found it already filled with beautiful dresses—and all of them were her size! There were dresses woven from the finest silks and dresses set with jewels. *Oh, I can't wait to wear all of these!* Gwen thought.

A knocking on her door distracted her from her new wardrobe.

"Who is it?" she called.

"It's me," Dev answered.

Immediately, all of Gwen's cranky feelings returned. "What?" she asked, opening the door.

"I…I just wanted to say good night."

"Good night," Gwen replied, and started to shut the door.

But Devin stuck out his arm and held it open. "What I mean is, I know you don't want me here, and I'm sorry if I upset you. Could we call a truce—at least for tonight?"

Gwen felt herself softening. Devin hated to go to bed when either one of them was angry at the other. He said it kept him awake all night. The truth was, she didn't like it much either.

Gwen held out her hand and grinned at her brother. "Truce," she said.

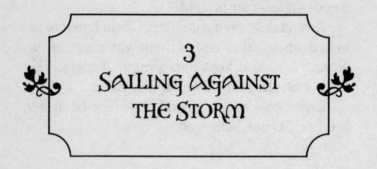

3
SAILING AGAINST
THE STORM

Devin's bed was rocking back and forth when he woke. Where was he? This wasn't his bedroom in London or even his little room in St. Ives. He blinked and then remembered that he was on board a ship bound for foreign lands.

The Lands of Legend. Trust Gwen to find a ship that would actually sail to the place. If he hadn't seen those gremlins and dwarves, he'd have thought it was all an elaborate game. But this ship was real. He didn't need an artist's imagination to know that.

Devin got up and looked around his cabin. It was rather ingenious, he had to admit. The furnishings were well built and useful, with many drawers, cupboards, and shelves in which to tuck everything away. The bed was plain but comfortable, and he wished he had such a bed back home. Even magical dwarves, it seemed, were more practical than the Thornworths. The closets here were filled with clothes that seemed to be about his size—handy things like trousers all covered with pockets, waxed rain gear, and good walking boots. He didn't want to impose on his hosts, however, by claiming these things for himself. He kept on the wrinkled clothes he had slept in and combed back his hair with his fingers.

Outside his room, the ship's hallway seemed to be an endless labyrinth. The place was vast, with countless rooms, both large and small and of every description. One cabin looked like a princess's bower (no doubt where his sister had slept last night); another had pillows, thick rugs, and draperies like a sultan's palace; the next three resembled a gypsy caravan, a wigwam, and a pirate's lair. Devin passed a grand ballroom, a billiards room, a room full of cats (all staring at him), a busy dining hall, a theater (where several gremlins were performing magic tricks), and finally he found the stairway that led to the deck of the *Basset*. As he stepped out into the sharp sea air, the *Basset* seemed to shrink in size. Out here on the deck, it was quite a small ship with no hint of the wonders below.

The sky was clear and bright this morning, and the sea held the old ship gently. A steady

wind filled the white sails and rippled the banner:
CREDENDO VIDES.

Sebastian sat in a sheltered spot, his breakfast on a small folding table. "Good morning," he
said when he spied the boy. "They're serving
breakfast in the dining hall. Miss Gwenevere is
there with the others."

"But you prefer to eat up here?" asked Devin.
"You certainly have a fine view."

The old dwarf flushed. "I'm still in disgrace.
Captain Malachi scowls whenever he sees me."

"May I join you, then? I'm in disgrace, too."

Sebastian gave the boy a measured look, then
nodded. "Your sister is wrong, you know. The
Basset must have wanted you. The gremlins
wouldn't have set sail with you on board if you
weren't meant to come."

He's just trying to make me feel better, Devin
thought. He didn't belong on a magical ship any
more than he belonged in a magical family.
Nonetheless, he would try to make himself useful to the dwarves and to Gwen.

A swarm of gremlins appeared on the deck,
tumbling over one another like kittens. One took
off his hat and pulled a whole chair out of it for
the boy to sit on. Another produced a bowl of
soup and a teapot in the same manner.

"Give him a teacup, a saucer, and a spoon,"
Sebastian reminded them. The spoon was

quickly produced, but the cup and saucer proved more difficult. A vase appeared, then a frying pan, a cookery book, and a croquet mallet. Finally, Devin was given an enormous cup decorated with mermaids.

Harpy soup, as Sebastian called it, made an odd but tasty breakfast. They talked as they ate, and Devin was soon held spellbound by the sailor's tales about the *Basset,* the Lands of Legend, and the history of the dwarvian race. He began to relax, comforted by the first mate's kindness and evident competence. The *Basset,* it seemed, would escort them all the way to the Faery Queen's island realm. But then, he discovered to his alarm, it would drop them off and sail away.

"We're late now, you see," Sebastian explained. "Due to that wretched Hepzibah affair. We picked him up entirely by mistake, and the gremlins nearly mutinied. Now there's a lonely old woman in Ireland who is overdue for an adventure. We'll pick her up and deliver her to the court of immortals on Tir-na-nog, and then we'll come back for you and Miss Gwenevere in a fortnight."

"A fortnight!" Devin exclaimed. His parents would worry dreadfully.

"Roughly. It will seem but a short time to those back in St. Ives," the old dwarf assured him.

Devin was relieved by this. His parents might never know they had gone—provided he managed to get Gwen back from the faeries in one piece.

"Can you tell me about the faeries?" he asked. "I don't quite know what to expect."

The sailor took out a wooden pipe and filled its bowl with dried herbs. "No one quite knows what to expect from the faeries. They're a bit...unpredictable. How much do you know about them, boy? Ever seen one in London or Cornwall?"

"Faeries? No!"

"They live there, too. 'Believing is seeing,' remember."

"I've never believed," Devin admitted. "I guess I'm going to have to now. But I know a little bit about them, from King Arthur tales and Shakespeare's plays. Gwen thinks faeries are all wonderful and beautiful and romantic. But in Shakespeare, Titania and Oberon quarrel and play wicked tricks on each other. In Arthurian tales, some of the faeries are good—like the Lady of the Lake, who gives Arthur his magical sword. But other faeries are dangerous, like the one who traps Merlin in a tree."

"You're a perceptive lad," said Sebastian. "So was young Will Shakespeare, I recall—always asked a million questions, like you, when he came on board. I'll give you the same advice that I gave to Will. This ship has an excellent library—one of the very best, I believe, outside of the College of Magical Knowledge. We have many books about the faeries, including my grandfather's classic work, *Faeries: Their Habits and Habitats,* all sixty-three volumes. I'll take you to the library after breakfast. You'll find a world of wisdom in books. But eat up first. Our harpies are excellent cooks, but they're prone to temper tantrums if you don't appreciate their food."

Devin ate. He didn't need harpies mad at him—Gwenevere was bad enough. She scowled when she climbed onto the deck and found him breakfasting with Sebastian. Then she tossed back her hair, attempted a smile, and said good morning.

"Morning," Dev said quietly, looking down at his fingers.

"The captain says we have a full day's travel ahead of us," she reported. "But if the wind is with us, I'll reach the Faery Queen's island tomorrow."

"Good," said Devin. "That gives me time to spend in the library today."

"The *library?*" said Gwen, incredulous. "You're planning to spend your day on board a magical ship with your nose in a book? You don't have to read about adventures—you're on one! Or hadn't you noticed, Dev?"

He flushed. His sister had a point. "I want to know more about these faeries," he mumbled. "To see what we're getting ourselves into…"

"We? You're planning to follow me onto the faeries' island, too? I should have known." Gwenevere looked cross again, and she tossed her hair some more. "I'd rather meet the faeries myself then learn about them from some musty book."

"Knowledge is always useful, miss," the first mate cautioned her.

"*Useful.* That's a Devin word. *Useful. Reasonable. Practical.* But I'm on my grand adventure, and I'm leaving all those stuffy words at home! You should, too," she said to Devin more gently, perhaps recalling their truce. "We're off to the Lands of Legend now. Let's be like the captain describes the gremlins: *creative, intuitive, impulsive,* and *utterly magical!*"

With each of these four descriptions, a grinning gremlin appeared at her side. One held a jeweled dress of azure blue, one held an ivory darning needle, one held a spool of thread, and one held something tied with a velvet ribbon.

"Mama's painting!" Gwenevere gasped. "What do you think you're doing with that?"

She made a grab for the canvas, but the gremlin evaded her easily, climbing up the *Basset*'s mast with the painting under his arm.

"Come down!" Gwen insisted, hands on her hips.

The gremlins cheerfully ignored her. The other three followed the first, perching together on the yardarm. Devin shaded his eyes against the sun to see what the gremlins were doing up there. They unrolled the painting, spread out the dress, unwound the thread...and started to sew. When they were done, they brought the dress to Gwen, bowed, and fled the deck, giggling from start to finish through the entire operation.

"Look at this!" his sister fumed. She carried the dress over to Sebastian. The azure blue dress seemed no different to Devin, its heavy skirt still encrusted with gems, its bodice embroidered with flowers and pearls. But then Gwen turned the skirt inside out, and there was the Aislings' portrait. The gremlins had sewn the canvas onto the underskirt with neat little stitches. The painting hadn't been harmed, but Gwen was outraged. "Devin, I need scissors!"

"Wait," said Sebastian. "Stop and think for a moment. The gremlins often do queer things, but there's usually a strange kind of logic at work. If they think the painting ought to be sewn into your skirt, perhaps they are right."

"But what a deucedly odd thing to do!" Gwen replied. (That was Papa's favorite expression.) She looked at the dress, considering. "At least it would leave my hands free to carry my valise and a lantern, as well. Is it far from the shore to the Faery Queen's court?"

"The distance changes with each traveler. But it can be a long and perilous road," Sebastian warned her.

Oh, great, thought Devin. A perilous road— and the *Basset* was off to Ireland. If Gwen thought she was setting foot on that island alone, she was daft.

"Perhaps they just want to protect Mama's painting from rain," mused Gwen, looking up at the clouds.

Devin blinked. Only a moment before, he would have sworn the summer sky had been clear. Now, dark clouds scudded overhead. A storm was definitely brewing.

"Oh, dear," said the first mate, following his gaze. "I think you had better go belowdecks. These seas can be rough—but HMS *Basset* is sound, miss. No need for alarm."

"I wasn't alarmed," said Gwen stoutly. "Devin will worry for both of us." Nonetheless, she hastened to go belowdecks, clutching the azure blue dress.

Her brother paused. "What can I do to help?" he asked the sailor. Despite his words to Gwen, Sebastian was looking distinctly worried.

Sebastian frowned, considering. "Go read

about the faeries, lad. There's something unnatural about this storm—I fear it may have come from them. Learn everything about the faery realm that you can. And, Master Devin," the dwarf added, his callused hand on the human boy's wrist. "There's nothing wrong with an orderly mind. It takes both the dwarves and the gremlins to run this ship. The gremlins can't do it alone."

Devin nodded and ducked inside. The sailor was trying to be kind again. Dwarves were practical *and* magical. Devin was just practical. But practicality was a quality Gwen would need, although she would never admit it. And so he was going to tag along, no matter how much she complained.

All through the day and into the night, the storm lashed against the boat, whipping up the waves and flooding the deck with a ferocious downpour. Yet belowdecks in the library, all was strangely quiet and calm. The floor rolled with the ship's motion, but the books stayed firmly in their place. The gas lamps on the wall barely flickered. Immersed in the volumes piled around him on the long mahogany library table, Devin was oblivious to the storm raging overhead.

Sebastian had been right: There were many books on these shelves about the faeries—and also about other creatures of myth and legend from around the world. The problem, however, was that each of the books seemed to want to tell him something different. One book said faeries were small as mice. The next one said no, they were tall as men. Half the volumes described the faeries as kind and helpful to humankind, while the other half insisted the faery court was treacherous. Even *Faeries: Their Habits and Habitats* proved to be of limited help—for the author, Sebastian Starblower the Fifth, changed his mind every few pages, contradicting himself all the way (as far as Devin could tell) through sixty-three volumes. The only thing all the books agreed on was the thing Sebastian (the Seventh) had told him: that faeries were unpredictable, particularly around humans.

Devin sighed, and closed another fat book. At least he'd gleaned a few basic facts. Faeries were nature spirits, he'd learned, and as such they could be found all over the world, appearing in many different guises and known by a wide variety of names. Titania and Oberon were English faeries, but there were many others, too—Cornish faeries, Italian faeries, Persian faeries, Japanese faeries, even Indian faeries in the wilds of the Americas. The rules of the Realm varied from place to place, but a few were universal. One was a ban on eating faery food, which could be quite dangerous. He'd have to speak to the harpies and pack some supplies to take with them tomorrow.

He made a list of other precautions: Don't talk about the faeries out loud unless you want to draw their attention. Don't try to bargain with them—they'll always outsmart you with some clever trick. Wearing your clothes inside out (he wrote down) gives you protection from faery mischief, as do iron nails in your coat pocket (faeries hate iron), a copper penny held under your tongue, henbane picked by the light of the moon, and salt on the windowsill. Crossing running water three times will lead you to the faery realm. Plants blooming out of season is a sign that you have found it.

All in all, these faeries sounded like very tricky characters. Queen Titania must be all right, for the Aisling sisters trusted her, and the dwarves of the *Basset* trusted the Aislings. But that didn't mean the entire faery island was perfectly safe. Devin remembered the grave look Miranda Aisling had given to Gwenevere. Of the two sisters, he'd bet *she* was the one who was practical, not Cassandra.

Devin flipped through the pages of *British Goblins* by a man with the funny name of Wirt Sikes. (He never noticed that the publication date of the book was 1880, six years in the future. The library of HMS *Basset* was magical indeed.) Here were more goblins, more faeries, more warnings against faery tricks, illusions, and mischief. He found himself yawning and checked his pocket watch. It was midnight. No wonder he was so tired! He'd been reading and writing for hours. It seemed like years since the gremlins had brought him his supper on a silver tray.

Suddenly, the boy heard a howling sound that made his hair stand on end. The ship was rolling. The gas lights sputtered. The storm seemed to be getting worse. Footsteps pounded down the hall, and the library door opened with a crash. Gwen ran into the room, her cambric nightdress billowing yards of lace.

"Devin," she said breathlessly, "did you hear that?"

Before he could say yes, he had, the dreadful howling started again, echoing throughout the ship.

"What on earth is it?" Gwen asked, her face pale.

"It could be the faeries," Devin warned. "Sebastian thinks they sent the storm. I've just been reading about them, and—"

"Bosh!" Gwen interrupted him. "The faeries wouldn't harm us, Dev. And I'm quite sure that faeries don't *howl*."

Devin didn't try to contradict her (he recognized her stubborn look)—but he'd just been reading about Tempest Faeries, who delighted in thunderstorms and gales. A third howl arose, and Gwen took her brother's hand, squeezing it hard.

"Is everything all right in here?" The ship's bosun appeared at the door. "The gremlins said they saw the young mistress running and looking distressed."

"I'm fine," Gwen insisted, despite a trembling voice, "but, but...what is that sound, Eli?"

"The howling, miss? That's the Minotaur. He's another guest of ours. The storm, it makes him seasick. Don't pay it any mind."

"Oh. I see." Gwen took a deep breath and let go of Devin's hand.

"The weather is bound to clear eventually, miss. Don't worry," said Eli kindly. He bobbed in a funny little bow and left the doorway.

Gwen attempted to toss her hair, but Devin could see she had been badly shaken. "I'm sure the bosun is right," she said firmly, as though to convince herself. "Perhaps we'll have better weather tomorrow. In fact, I'll go and imagine it now. *Credendo vides.* I'll use my imagination and then it will happen."

As she turned to go, she suddenly stopped and looked more closely at her twin. She had the expression on her face that Papa had named the "bird eye." This was a particular look of Gwen's—her head cocked to one side while she peered at you out of one dark eye. It made her look just like the raven in the tapestry over her bed.

"Dev," she said, "you look terrible. There are big black shadows under your eyes. I think I ought to take you back to your cabin. You need some sleep."

"I'll go to bed soon," he promised her. "I've one more book I want to check—"

"No more books. Just look at you! You're practically asleep in that chair. Come on, now."

Gwen tugged at his arm and pulled him up and out of the chair. Devin meekly followed her—partly because he was so tired, and partly because he was so surprised to find her mothering him like this. Did this mean that they'd reversed their roles, and *he'd* be bold and creative now? He smiled as she left him at his door. Somehow, he doubted it.

Dev was so tired that he was fast asleep as soon as his head hit the pillow. A moment later (it seemed), a crack of thunder woke him up. According to an ingenious dwarvian clock on the wall, it was morning already. The boy sat up, stretched, then jumped from the bed. He felt remarkably good. There was something magical about this bed. He'd never slept so well.

Devin straightened his wrinkled clothes as

best he could and borrowed a waxed rain cape. (Sebastian had assured him that these things had been provided for his use.) Then he made his way through the labyrinthine halls to the stairs leading up to the deck. A burly dwarf was coming down, water streaming from his beard.

"Stay belowdecks," the seaman said. "You'd be washed overboard out there in the squall."

So Devin made for the dining hall instead. He found Sebastian there, drinking tea at the captain's table. Clearly, their quarrel was over.

"Master Thornworth," called Captain Malachi, "come join us at the high table. Your sister is with our helmsman, determined to wish a blue sky into existence—and perhaps she will! I'd hoped to reach the faeries' island by noon, but the wind is not going to let us. Nonetheless, the *wuntarlabe* tells us to persist—so persist we shall."

Devin was actually sorry to hear this—he had secretly hoped they would have to turn back. But it seemed that the dwarves, the *Basset,* and the *wuntarlabe* were as stubborn as Gwen.

The storm battered the boat throughout the day. Even in the library, protected from the worst of the storm, Devin began to feel as green as the seasick Minotaur. And then, as suddenly as they had come, the wind and rain simply disappeared. The ocean calmed, the boat rocked gently, and

Devin made his way to the deck. Outside, the air was fresh and sweet. Sunlight sparkled on the wet rigging. Sebastian pointed, and Devin could see dry land on the western horizon.

The sun was poised just above the trees, spreading a golden evening light when the *Basset* sailed into the empty harbor of the faery island. It was a beautiful but lonely place—wild, deserted, and utterly still. There were only silent trees to greet them, beyond a sandy beach. The anchor was lowered (in a tussle between Bosun Eli and a half dozen gremlins), and a launch was prepared to take the passengers to shore.

Gwen was full of herself this evening, having stopped the great storm single-handedly (or so she firmly believed). She wore the magnificent gem-encrusted dress, ready for her meeting with the Queen. Captain Malachi shook their hands in farewell, then the first mate took the children aside. Sebastian's face was rather grave, and he spoke to them in an urgent tone.

"We'd hoped to drop you off at noon. Now it is dusk—a treacherous time. You must always be wary of faeries at twilight. All doors to the Realm stand open then."

"But that's just what we want," said Gwen, delighted. Nothing could daunt her now.

"Ah, but will you enter the right door? No, little maid, listen to me. I see that your brother is

paying attention. Dusk, as I said, is a treacherous
time—and darkness can be even worse. Make a
camp. You are safe here on the beach. Mermaids
will watch over you. By morning light, you can
find your way to Titania and Oberon's court."

"But all we've been doing is eating and sleep-
ing and waiting," Gwen protested. "I'm ready to
go!"

"Patience, miss. Just one more night, then
you'll find the land of your heart's desire. You've
waited twelve years—what's one night more?"

"Oh, I suppose," said Gwen with a sigh.

"The harpies have packed a supper for us,"
Dev said brightly to distract his twin. "Just think
how perfectly romantic and artistic it will be
tonight. You've brought your paints, haven't you?
I'll light a fire, make some tea, and spread our
bedrolls on the beach. We'll watch the mermaids
swim by the light of the moon. Wouldn't Nanny
Swan have a fit!"

Devin's ploy worked. The girl's face brightened. She asked, "Will we really see mermaids,
Sebastian?"

"Of course," the old sailor replied. He leaned
close to Devin's ear and whispered, "Don't you
worry, Master Devin. I'll have a word with them,
and they'll dance and sing to your heart's con-
tent. But keep her here till the morrow. No doubt
Titania will send for you."

"Thank you, sir," Devin replied, sorry to let the old dwarf go. Hearing his tales had been the best part of the journey, at least for Devin. "When will we see the *Basset* again?"

"When the *wuntarlabe* brings us back this way. Don't worry, lad. You'll have a great adventure. Just trust your imagination."

"He hasn't got one," Gwen said, grinning. "Good thing I've got enough for two."

Devin wasn't hurt—she was teasing him now. She put her arm through his and laughed. "Oh, isn't it wonderful, Dev? Just wait till we tell the others back home!"

They said their good-byes and climbed down to the launch. A small pack of gremlins rowed them to shore. One pulled a bundle from his hat and presented it to Devin.

"For me?" he asked shyly. The gremlin nodded, his top hat bobbing over his eyes.

"I hope it's clothes. You need them," said Gwen. "Something dashing, heroic, and colorful! You can't look ordinary and drab when we meet the Faery Queen."

We, she had said. Devin smiled. He was really part of this journey now. He helped the gremlins pull the boat ashore and unload their gear on the sand: Gwen's valise, Devin's new pack (courtesy of Captain Malachi), the dinner basket, two bedrolls, and the gremlin's mysterious bundle.

The launch returned to the *Basset* as the twins hauled their gear farther up the beach, close to the shadow of the brooding trees—but not too close.

Soon the tide would turn again, the ship would be off, and they'd be alone...Devin looked through the thickening dusk toward the ship. It seemed small and distant.

"So let's see what the gremlins gave us," Gwen said gaily, untying the strings and belts and buckles that held the bundle together. She gave a shriek as it came undone, coming to life and jumping from her hands. In a flurry of motion, a tent erected itself on the sand before them. It was quite a grand and exotic thing, like something King Arthur's knights might have used. In fact, Papa had put a tent very much like this in one of his paintings.

Gwen looked at it with shining eyes. "Oh, how magical!" she breathed.

"Magical *and* practical," said Devin with satisfaction.

"Well, here's something practical I can do," Gwen announced, her hands on her hips. "I'll gather driftwood for a fire. I know you," she added, teasing again. "You'll want a nice cup of tea."

He grinned at her. "Excellent idea. Before it's dark and we can't see a thing."

Gwen promptly set off down the beach while Devin unpacked the kettle and cups. As he searched through his pack for matches, he heard his sister calling his name.

"Devin, Devin, look! In the trees! Old stone ruins, statues, broken columns—covered with ivy and moss. It looks like it used to be an old temple, but everything's overgrown now."

He looked where she pointed. Something gleamed very white in the shadows of oak and ash. "We'll explore it all tomorrow," he called back. "Remember Sebastian's warning."

He found matches, a water jug, and a tin of tea labeled UNICORN'S BEST.

"Dev, look!" Gwen called again.

He sighed and turned. She was pointing toward the woods. He squinted, puzzled, and then saw it—little lights that flickered through the dusk.

Devin laughed, relieved. It was fireflies. Nothing to worry about. But Gwen was running toward the lights. Straight into the dark of the trees.

"Gwen, wait!" he yelled, alarmed.

"Look! They're amazing. You've got to see—"

She entered the trees, and the darkness swallowed her up. And the lights disappeared.

4
THE DARK QUEEN'S COURT

"Gwen, wait!" Devin shouted.

But Gwen barely heard her brother's call. She was fascinated by the lights. They hovered over the old stone ruins and darted between the trees. They danced against the dusk—gold, green, and deep blue. They reminded her of the golden ball in the tapestry in her room. They looked like jewels against the darkening sky. They were—she was sure of it—pure magic.

If only she could hold one, even for a second. The lights formed rings and then stars. They circled each other, tumbled from branches, and played what looked like a game of tag. One light, a golden one, seemed to move a little more slowly than the others. Gwen followed it deeper into the forest. She had the sense that it knew she was following, that it wanted her to. The golden light danced from bluebells to ivy to pale tiger lilies. Gwen chased after it, paying no mind to where her feet were going—and quite suddenly felt her foot catch on a thick root and the rest of her go flying through the air.

She landed with a very undignified *squush* on a patch of soft, boggy ground. She lay still for a moment, then realizing she wasn't hurt, picked herself up.

"Eeew!" She removed a green worm from her hair and wriggled her toes. Her shoes were filled with muddy water. She glanced down at herself. "Oh, my beautiful dress!" she wailed.

The azure blue dress was covered with brownish green mud. Worse, the front of the jeweled dress, where the gremlins had sewn Mama's painting into the lining, was soaked through. *Oh, I do hope the painting isn't ruined,* Gwen thought worriedly. *How will I ever explain this to Titania? Or Mama? Or the Aisling sisters?*

She pulled a broad leaf from a nearby tree and tried to wipe the mud from her skirts—but succeeded mainly in smearing it around. Then she heard something that sounded like laughter. Except that it wasn't. *If a crystal bell could laugh, that's exactly what it would sound like,* she thought. She glanced around, but the marvelous golden light was gone.

Something nipped her hand, hard.

"Ow!" cried Gwen. She suddenly had the horrid feeling that she'd been chasing glowing, biting insects.

A tiny violet light hovered over her hand and nipped her again.

Gwen was about to swat it when the violet light came to rest on the center of her palm. Gwen raised her hand for a better look and stared in disbelief. She was holding a tiny, perfectly formed woman. Delicate wings set with amethysts fluttered on her back. She wore a violet gossamer dress and had long, flowing violet hair, and eyes that flashed violet light.

"Moon and stars," Gwen breathed. "You're a faery!"

The faery smiled, revealing sharp pointed teeth. "You thought I was a bug."

"Only because you bit me," Gwen told her.

The faery crossed her delicate arms and glared.

Gwen realized that she'd gotten off to a bad start. "I'm sorry," she added quickly. "I didn't mean to be rude. It's just that I've never met a faery before."

"Well, now you have." The faery still sounded huffy. "You're very lucky for a mortal, you know. We usually don't show ourselves to your kind. Especially when they're so muddy."

Gwen felt herself blush with embarrassment.

"Oh, I *know,* and I'm *so* grateful," she said quickly. "You see, ever since I was a little girl, I've wanted to meet faeries."

The tiny creature smiled her feral smile. "You have? Why?"

"Because I'm an artist," Gwen explained. "Everyone in my family is, except for my brother. And we've all been drawing and painting your realm for years."

"Our realm, indeed. What a coincidence," said the violet faery. "Well, then, you must know a good deal about us."

"Not nearly as much as I'd like to," Gwen admitted. "Though, deep down, I've always known that my life would be filled with magic and enchantment."

The faery stood up, yawned, and stretched. "Well, then, child of magic, it would be rude of me to do anything but lead you to your destiny."

Gwen hesitated for a moment, not quite sure of what the faery meant. Perhaps it was up to her to be clear. "I would like to meet Titania and Oberon," she said. "Can you take me to them?"

The faery's eyes flashed violet sparks. "I will take you to the Faery Queen herself," she promised.

Gwen was so happy she would have turned cartwheels if she hadn't feared that it might somehow offend the violet faery. She'd already figured out that faeries were extremely sensitive creatures.

She felt the lightest pressure on her palm—the violet faery springing off her hand and into the air. "We should go then," the faery told her. "Night has fallen, and mortals don't do well in this forest at night."

The girl blinked in surprise. She hadn't realized it was so late. But the faery was right. The sun was gone, and so were the other faery lights. It was as though a black velvet curtain covered the forest. Gwen could barely make out the trees. For a second, she wondered where Devin and the tent were. Dev should have a lantern lit by now, but if he did, Gwen couldn't see it from where she was. She couldn't even hear the sound of the sea anymore.

"What are you waiting for?" the violet faery demanded.

"Nothing," Gwen answered. "It's just so... odd. The forest feels different than it did before. It doesn't even feel like we're still on the island."

The faery made an impatient little squawk. "Save your artistic impressions for later," she ordered. "Or you can forget about meeting the Faery Queen."

"No, I'm coming," Gwen assured her.

The violet faery was already flying through the forest. Gwen hurried to keep her in sight.

Bushes pulled at her dress. Branches scratched at her face. Once, she almost ran into a tree. It occurred to her that Dev would probably be worried sick by now. She hadn't even told him she was going off. Then again, she couldn't possibly find her brother in the dark, so it was really much more sensible for her to follow the violet faery.

As soon as I find the Faery Court, I shall ask someone to go fetch Dev, she told herself.

The faery flew on ahead of her. Gwen followed the glowing violet light, losing all sense of time and distance. She had no idea whether they traveled a long time or short, whether they covered a few yards or many miles. All she knew was that the other faeries had vanished, and the violet faery was dancing ahead of her, the only glimmer of light in the island's dark night.

At last, Gwen could make out the land rising in a steep wooded hill. The faery hovered before it.

"Are we here?" Gwen asked breathlessly.

"I thought you'd recognize it. You must have heard the stories—the wee folk frolicking under the hill? Just what is it that you and your artist family have been drawing all these years?"

The faery's mocking tone made Gwen glad of the darkness, glad no one could see her turning scarlet with embarrassment.

"Actually," Gwen explained, "my father and mother and sisters—and I—we like to put our faeries in the woods, or on the shores of a lake, or sometimes in gloomy, old castles."

The faery landed on the end of Gwen's nose and gave it a tweak. "How very kind!"

Gwen rubbed her nose. *Now* what had she done? She certainly hoped the other faeries weren't this temperamental.

The violet faery began to beat her gossamer wings together, and Gwen heard a series of light, bell-like chimes. As if in answer to the song, a rectangle of turf fell away from the hill, revealing a door of carved rock crystal.

The crystal door swung open. The violet fairy extended her hand. "Welcome, mortal," she said. "It is not often we get such guests."

Gwen's pulse raced with excitement as she stepped through the door. This was the moment she'd been dreaming of her entire life! Inside, she found a cramped, narrow tunnel carved into the hill. Its earthen walls were webbed with exposed tree roots, and from between them, tiny, dirt-smudged faces peered out at her.

"More faeries!" Gwen exclaimed with delight.

The violet faery feigned a look of astonishment. "Fancy that! You found faeries in the Realm! How utterly extraordinary!"

"Well, it is for me," Gwen said a bit defensively. "I'm not used to seeing your kind."

"You will be," the violet faery promised. "You, my girl, are about to see more faeries than you ever dreamed existed."

Gwen continued through the tunnel, thinking it was really a rather dark and dingy place for such fantastic creatures to live. The earth of the hill smelled musty and a bit moldy, and the air was thick and heavy. She was relieved when the tunnel opened into a long, high-ceilinged corridor. Torches blazed from the walls, and she saw that the violet faery had told the truth. The hall was thronged with faeries—or, at least, otherworldly creatures. Gwen didn't mean to gape, but these faeries were not what she'd expected. They weren't all tiny and pretty like the violet faery. They came in every shape and size—tall and slender as reeds, or roly-poly as pumpkins. Some had skeletal wings, others webbed feet. Still others had pointed ears and pale green skin. Some were frighteningly ugly, like creatures from Gwen's most horrific nightmares. All of them watched her with glittering eyes. And all of them had that same feral smile.

Gwen did her best to smile back. "Hello," she said politely as she followed the violet faery through the corridor. "Delighted to be here. Lovely to meet you."

None of them answered her, though she

caught the words "mortal girl" and "filthy dress" being whispered.

The corridor ended in a steep, winding stairway that was carved of stone. "This way, mortal," the violet faery said, flying upward.

Gwen soon wished that she, too, could fly. The stairs were a chore to climb, worse even than the hill from the waterfront in St. Ives. Each step was at least a foot high, and they seemed to go on forever. Gwen climbed and climbed. Though she could no longer see the torchlit corridor below, she seemed no closer to the top than she had been at the start.

The violet faery, who'd disappeared from view, darted down and hovered near Gwen's right ear. "Hurry up, girl!" she said, giving Gwen's ear a sharp tug. "You're slow!"

"Well, I'd be a lot faster if I had wings!" Gwen replied indignantly, but the annoying little creature had already flown from sight.

Gwen was panting by the time she finally reached the top of the stairs. Still, she was so grateful to find that there *was* a top to the stairs that she really didn't mind. Especially when she realized that she was now standing in the most extraordinary chamber she had ever seen. It was a huge airy high-ceilinged room. The floor was tiled with silver and gold and studded with gems. The walls were carved ruby and glittered blood red in the torchlight. Rows of golden columns led to the front of the room, where a golden throne sat on a silver platform.

Once again, Gwen found herself surrounded by faeries. Here, though, they ignored her so completely that she wondered if she were invisible. They all were talking among themselves quite intently, and she got the impression that matters of great importance were being discussed. Only the violet faery paid her any attention, occasionally flying back and nudging her toward the throne.

A sudden flurry of wings sounded, and the faeries fell silent. Gwen stared in wonder as a flock of ravens swooped into the throne room. They circled the great hall, then perched on top of the golden columns—except for one exceedingly large raven who settled on the throne.

The violet faery pinched Gwen's arm. "Bow!" she whispered, and Gwen realized that a tall, magnificent woman now stood in front of the throne. She had ivory skin, fine high-boned features, and golden eyes. A thin golden circlet glittered in her black hair, which hung loose over a gleaming black silk gown. Two long coal black wings were folded behind her back. Gwen could not take her eyes off her. Somehow, she'd never imagined Titania looking quite like this.

The violet faery pinched Gwen's arm again. "Have you no manners?"

"Oh!" Gwen said, startled. Instinctively, she dropped into a deep curtsy.

The violet faery pinched her harder. "I said *bow!*"

"Leave her be." The Faery Queen spoke in a rich, melodious voice. "The mortal child is not used to our ways. Come here, girl. Let me have a look at you."

The throng of faeries parted, and the girl made her way toward the Faery Queen. She wished desperately that she wasn't covered in mud. And she wondered how she was going to explain what had happened to her mother's painting. Perhaps it was better not to mention it until she'd had a chance to look it over and repair any damage.

As Gwen neared the dais, the Queen seated herself on the high golden throne. The throne had no back—allowing for the Queen's wings—but its armrests were carved in the shape of two kneeling deer. Gwen had never seen such exquisite carving. If the deer hadn't been made of gold, she would have expected them to breathe.

A line of courtiers stood on each side of the Queen. These were tall, slender, handsome creatures, each holding a long silver lance. All except for one. He was by far the handsomest and the most slender of the lot, with dark, remote eyes that seemed to gaze into another world entirely.

"So, mortal child." The Queen's voice distracted Gwen from the handsome courtier. "Do you have a name?"

"Gwenevere Thornworth," Gwen replied.

"What happened to your dress, Gwenevere?" the Queen asked, not unkindly.

"I fell into a bog," Gwen confessed in a small voice.

"It's no matter," the Queen told her. "I will have a chamber with a change of clothing prepared for you."

"Thank you," Gwen said, feeling a bit better.

One of the ravens flew down from its column and perched on the Queen's shoulder, a gesture that Gwen found even more reassuring. It reminded her of the tapestry in her room.

"And I will have a good hot supper sent to you," the Faery Queen went on. "You look as though it's been a while since your last meal."

"Yes, it has been. Thank you," Gwen said. She was feeling bolder now. It was really only the violet faery who was unpleasant. Titania was quite gracious.

The Queen regarded her through narrowed golden eyes. "I'm told you have an interest in our kind. Which, naturally, makes me curious about you—so many mortals no longer even believe we exist. Tell me, human child, are you a musician, by any chance?"

"A musician?" Gwen said, startled.

"Yes, I am very fond of music, and thought that perhaps you might play an instrument or sing."

"I'm afraid not," Gwen said, hoping she wasn't disappointing the Faery Queen. "But I am an artist. From a family of artists. And we all love nothing better than drawing the Faery Realm and magical heroes and heroines. We know quite a lot about King Arthur and—"

The Queen raised one slender hand, and Gwen stopped.

"I'm sure that's all very interesting." The Faery Queen sounded bored. "Why don't you get some rest now, and we'll discuss things in the morning? Violet Faery, show her to her room."

Gwen felt her heart sink. Didn't Titania believe her? She knew that faeries adored talented mortals. Well, she would just have to show her. If only she hadn't left her art supplies on the beach.

"Please, Your Highness," Gwen spoke up quickly. "Could I have some canvas and some paints?"

The Faery Queen looked at her with curiosity.

"Whatever for?"

"Painting pictures...It's what I do."

The Queen waved a hand at the violet faery. "See that the mortal child has what she needs," she instructed. Then she turned and gazed at the young courtier who had no lance.

"Do *you* paint?" she asked him mockingly.

"No," he replied, looking straight ahead.

Gwen bit back a gasp of surprise. He wasn't another faery. He was human!

"You really don't do much of anything, do you?" the Queen taunted him.

"I told you," he said stiffly. "I'm a traveler."

"Then you are of little use to me," the Queen snapped. Gwen felt her heart pounding. She couldn't bear it if Titania spoke to her with such contempt. She would have to paint something absolutely gorgeous. Perhaps a portrait of the Faery Queen herself.

Violet Faery yanked on Gwen's hair. "You've been dismissed!" she scolded. "Now bow to the Lady and move out of the way! She has more important business to attend to."

Gwen did as she was told, but silently resolved that the next morning—when Titania realized what a wonderful artist she was—she would tell the Faery Queen just how rudely she'd been treated.

The violet faery led Gwen through a door on

the side of the throne room to a narrow corridor that wound through the earth like a mole's tunnel. This one was even dingier and more cramped than the entrance to the hill. It twisted and branched and turned back on itself so many times that Gwen was soon hopelessly confused. She couldn't tell if they'd gone right or left, up or down, or simply traveled endlessly in circles.

At last, they came to a small wooden door. Violet Faery hovered at the latch and pushed the door open. "Inside," she ordered Gwen. "I'll come for you in the morning."

The faery slammed the door shut, leaving Gwen alone in a small dim room that was lit by a single candle. "Oh," she said, trying to suppress a surge of disappointment. After the delightful room on the *Basset* and the grandeur of the Faery Queen's throne room, she'd somehow expected more. This room was very simple, furnished with a bed, a tiny wooden table and chair, and a wardrobe so narrow that it couldn't have held more than one dress. Still, all the woodwork was intricately carved with animal designs, and a meal that smelled heavenly was set out on the table.

Gwen was starving. She sat down at the table and devoured the meal, which consisted of some sort of meat, some sort of boiled root, and a thick-crusted bread. The odd thing was that the food didn't have much taste. Still, it filled her empty stomach, and she finished it all, though she couldn't help remembering how delicious the *Basset*'s harpy soup had been. It suddenly occurred to her that she'd forgotten all about Dev and hadn't asked anyone to fetch him. She hoped he wasn't too terribly worried.

I'll ask first thing in the morning, Gwen resolved. *Now I must paint something wonderful.* She was determined to impress the Faery Queen. Glancing around, she saw that a few sheets of paper, a quill pen, and a bottle of ink were tucked away in a corner of the room. These were not at all what she'd requested—and they wouldn't help her fix any damage to Mama's painting. That, she decided, would have to wait until morning.

Gwen dipped the quill pen in the ink and made a few experimental lines on the paper. The paper was so thin that it nearly tore every time she touched the pen to it. "The least they could have done was given me some proper charcoal," she muttered.

She closed her eyes for a second, picturing the Faery Queen. Then she opened her eyes and began to draw. She started with the face—the high cheekbones, the golden eyes...

"Ugh!" Gwen said after a few minutes. The

drawing looked more like Nanny Swan than the Faery Queen.

She flexed her fingers. Maybe she ought to warm up with something a little easier, something in plain sight. She settled on a little mouse carved into the bedpost.

With the wooden mouse in front of her, Gwen worked more quickly. She outlined the pointed nose, the rounded ears, the little hunched body, and the long thin tail. Then she began to sketch in the whorls of fur, the delicate whiskers and paws.

Gwen yawned as she finished the drawing. She felt as though she'd been awake for days. She rubbed her bleary eyes. She still wanted to draw the Faery Queen, but maybe if she just lay down for a quick nap...

Gwen took off her muddy dress. Wearing only her camisole and petticoat, she stretched out beneath the scratchy wool blanket. The bed was hard and lumpy, rather like her own bed at home. As she let her eyes drift closed, she heard a faint high-pitched sound. Her eyes shot open. Were there mice in Titania's palace? Gwen sat up in bed. Sure enough, a tiny brown mouse pawed at the door of her room and then disappeared beneath it.

The Faery Queen needs a cat, was Gwen's last

thought before she fell into a deep, exhausted sleep.

Gwen woke to someone shaking her shoulder. *It's that bossy violet faery,* she thought groggily. But the voice that said, "Please wake up. I must speak with you!" was deep and male.

Gwen forced her eyes open and saw the handsome young mortal, sitting on the side of her bed. She immediately drew the blanket up to her chin. "What are you doing in here?" she demanded.

He put a finger to his lips. "Shhh. Please. I've just come to talk, but you must listen. It's urgent."

Gwen wasn't sure what she thought about this handsome stranger appearing in her room. Clearly, it wasn't proper. Titania probably wouldn't approve. On the other hand, Gwen was dying of curiosity to know why he'd come. "Speak quickly, then," she told him.

He nodded. "My name is Thomas the Rhymer. Despite what I told the Queen, I am a teller of tales and a singer of songs—someone who, like you, has always dreamed of the faery realm and wanted to find it."

"And isn't it fabulous?" Gwen couldn't help saying.

"Is it?" Thomas asked.

Gwen stared at him, not understanding.

"There are *two* faery courts," the Rhymer explained. "One, the Seelie Court, is the domain of Oberon and Titania, the faeries who aid and protect mortals. But you and I have stumbled into the Unseelie Court—the realm of the faeries who delight in plaguing mortals. They steal babies, send storms, destroy crops, and cause harm whenever possible."

"But Titania would never—"

"It is not Titania you met," Thomas said. "That was Nicnevin, the Raven Queen. Didn't you wonder where Oberon was?"

"I thought he was...out," Gwen said lamely. The truth was, she'd been so excited to meet the Faery Queen that she hadn't given much thought to the King.

"There is only one throne in that throne room, and it belongs to Nicnevin, the Dark Queen."

Gwen didn't want to believe that she'd stumbled into the wrong faery realm, but something in the tone of Thomas's voice began to stir her doubts. "That can't be...What makes you so sure?"

"Everything," Thomas told her. "Everything in this place is wrong. You can never tell if it's day or night. Every surface glitters, yet what lies underneath is a nightmare. Even the furniture"—he hit the bedpost—"is so wretchedly uncomfortable."

"Oh, that doesn't mean anything," Gwen said cheerfully. "All the furniture in my house is like that."

"Then it's a queer sort of house you've got," Thomas muttered.

"That's because we're artists," she explained. "All of us except my brother Dev, that is."

Amusement flickered in Thomas's dark eyes. "And what does this brother of yours do?"

Gwen had to think for a moment. "He sees to things," she said at last. "When there's something to be planned or fixed, Dev sees to it. He's terribly practical."

"Well, then, lucky we'd be if Dev were here," Thomas said. "I suspect neither you nor I would be in this place if we were a shade more practical."

The Rhymer looked so upset that Gwen felt obliged to cheer him up. "Look, I know the rooms are simple, but it's really not so bad to be Nicnevin's guests—"

"Guests?" Thomas echoed. "You must trust me on this. Nicnevin doesn't have guests. Every mortal creature here is her prisoner."

He's wrong about that, Gwen thought. "If we were prisoners, they would lock our doors," she argued. "But you seem to have left your room. And obviously my room wasn't locked, since you came right in."

"Why should they bother to lock doors?" Thomas asked her. "Do you really believe any mortal creature could find their way out of this maze of tunnels? They're not afraid of our escaping. Still, we must try."

Gwen thought about that. She rather liked the idea of escaping from the Unseelie Court with this handsome young singer. "Wonderful!" she said. "It will be a grand and exciting adventure!"

"We'll do our best," Thomas said. He sounded rather grim, and Gwen wondered if he was going to turn out to be a damp blanket, like her brother. "The first rule," he went on, "is that you must not eat any of the food they give you."

Gwen felt her stomach churning. "I—I already did," she told him. "It was suppertime. I was famished."

Thomas shut his eyes. "I tried to find you earlier," he said. "To warn you. But all the corridors here—I had no luck at all until the mouse found me."

"The mouse?"

Thomas opened his pocket, and a tiny brown face peered out. It looked awfully familiar. Gwen's eyes darted to the bedpost, and her mouth fell open. The mouse on the bedpost was gone!

"That's the mouse I drew!" she told the Rhymer. "I recognize that bent whisker!"

"Very likely," he agreed. "There's all sorts of strange magic at work here. Nothing is ever quite what it seems."

Gwen drew a breath for courage. "So...I've eaten their food. What does that mean?"

"That you can never leave the Realm," Thomas said quietly. "If you do, you'll weaken and waste away to nothing."

"Like you?" Gwen asked. It suddenly occurred to her that he was *too* thin.

Thomas gave a bitter laugh. "My problem is quite the opposite. I haven't eaten a thing since I found myself down here. I may be starving to death, but at least I'm not giving in to Nicnevin."

Gwen swallowed hard. "Then there's no chance of escape for me?"

A look of anguish came into the Rhymer's eyes. "Now that you've eaten the Dark Queen's food, none that I know of. I'm sorry, young Gwen, but you're bound to live out the rest of your life as a prisoner of the Raven Queen."

5
THE WHITE
QUEEN'S COURT

Devin spent a wretched night on the beach, wrapped in his bedroll against a cold wind and trying to stay awake in case there was any sign of his sister.

He had walked for what seemed like hours, searching the edge of the dark and silent woods. He couldn't go farther—the forest itself seemed determined to keep him out. No matter how long or far he walked, the beach was never far behind, as though the trees were shifting places and leading him in a circle. He had called and called, but only silence answered. The woods seemed to be empty of life. Even the fireflies were gone as he trudged slowly back to camp.

While a full moon crossed the vast foreign sky, Devin kept vigil by a campfire. Out at sea, the mermaids cavorted—golden and silver against the dark waves—with no idea that the one they were sent to enchant was no longer here.

The boy eventually nodded off as the fire burned out unnoticed beside him. He woke stiff, chilled, and sick with fear as sunrise broke over the sea. The pale pink light was beautiful, but Dev was in no mood for beauty. The lonely loveliness of the island seemed sinister now. The bay was empty. The *Basset* was gone to Ireland and Tir-na-nog. The mermaids had gone wherever mermaids go. He sighed miserably.

Stop that, Thornworth, he told himself briskly. Misery wouldn't help his sister. Perhaps she wasn't even in trouble—perhaps she'd simply gotten excited and run ahead to the court. Gwen was often impulsive like that. No doubt she was feeling guilty now and would soon persuade the Faery Queen to send a message to him.

Methodically, he re-lit the fire and heated the dinner they'd never eaten. He wanted to run and find Gwen right away, but that wouldn't be very sensible—first he'd eat to keep up his strength, then he'd pack up all of their gear and find a safe spot to stow it, and *then* he'd go look for his sister. He made himself eat the rich stew, barely tasting it, then rinsed out his bowl in a nearby stream. The large tent disassembled itself in a flurry of motion, wind, and sand. The boy soon had it buckled up and stowed (with Gwen's heavy valise) in a hollow space below some tree roots.

As the sun rose high, the day grew warm. The air took on a sweet, heady perfume, and the woods by day were not quite so threatening as they'd been by night. He followed the stream into the trees, and this time the forest let him in. Soon he was far from the beach and could no longer hear the soft slap of the waves.

The stream grew deep and wide as he walked, winding through oak and elder roots. The water ran clear, then foamed white as milk on black stones in a series of rapids. He seemed to be following a trail, narrow and badly overgrown, as though it had been a long, long time since any had passed this way. There was still no sign of Gwenevere—but the boy continued to hike upstream. He'd make his way to the faery court. That's where Gwen was bound to be. And when he saw her, he'd find out whether relief or anger would be stronger.

The trail led him to stepping-stones, and he crossed them to the stream's other bank. *That's once,* thought Devin. *When I've crossed running water three times, I'll find the faeries.* An hour later, he crossed the stream again on a bridge half buried in thorns. *That's twice,* he thought with satisfaction, and sat down beside the stream. He took off his pack, opened it, and found his collapsible drinking cup—a perfectly ingenious device he'd received from the clever dwarves. He also found a book he'd not noticed before, with a note inside the cover: *To Devin, may you find this volume of use, from your sensible friend, Sebastian.* The boy smiled as he opened the little book, barely bigger than his palm. The author was a Professor Aisling (the sisters' father, perhaps?), and the book seemed to be a traveler's journal. Sebastian had marked a few pages.

Devin read those pages with great interest. The professor had sailed on HMS *Basset* and traveled to this very isle—along with his daughters, Miranda and Cassandra, when the girls were young. The Aislings had followed a stream (this one?), encountered the faeries, and met Queen Titania. He read the professor's account eagerly while sipping the icy stream water. The water tasted like flowers and honey and seemed to fill him with new strength.

"Thank you, Sebastian," he said out loud as he pocketed the volume and stood. "You, too, Professor," he added, shouldering his pack once more. The book had explained what he could expect, and knowing that always made Devin feel better. On the other hand, Devin remembered, he was in the realm of the faeries now. And that meant he had better expect the unexpected, just in case.

If it hadn't been for his nagging worry about Gwen (*She's with Queen Titania,* he told himself firmly), Devin would have enjoyed this journey through the forest—so vast, dark, and untamed compared to the woodlands he'd known in Cornwall. The undergrowth was thick with flowers: foxglove, bluebells, and tiger lilies. Berries hung heavy on old rowan trees; walnuts and acorns lay underfoot. *Plants blooming out of season,* he remembered reading, *means the faeries are near.*

A waterfall should be just ahead if this was the stream the Aislings had followed. Soon he heard its roaring sound. Good. He was on the right path. This was where the professor had met...Devin rounded the bend and stopped in his tracks. The journal could not have prepared the boy for his first sight of the falls themselves, tumbling down a cliff that rose an impossible distance above. The water sheeted down golden stone and churned in the whirlpool far below. A flock of white birds hovered over the pool, their white wings luminous. Behind the falls was a cave. And in that cave lived a manticore.

Devin's stomach clenched, but in fact, he told himself, there was really nothing to fear. The manticore guarded the door that led to Titania and Oberon's court—but the monster ate only intruders. Devin would simply, politely explain why he had come to the faeries' realm. If Gwen was at the court already (*And surely she is,* he thought once again), then the beast might be expecting him—if the creature was even here anymore. Many years had gone by, after all, since the Aislings had passed this way.

The boy squared his shoulders. He had no choice. He needed to cross the stream a third time, and the only way was to climb onto the ledge that led behind the waterfall and out through the manticore's cave. He took a deep breath, picked up a stout stick (just in case politeness didn't suffice), and stepped up to the narrow ledge.

The stone was slippery with moss and crumbling at its farthest edge. Devin clung to the wall as he followed the ledge, passed behind the waterfall, and entered the gloom of the cave. A powerful stench pervaded the place, smelling sour, musky, and wild. As soon as the footing was sure underneath, he reached for the lantern that hung from his pack. He fumbled with matches, lit the wick—and gasped. Someone else gasped, too.

A woman was staring at him, alarmed, blinking in the sudden light.

"I'm ever so sorry to startle you..." the boy began to apologize, but his words trailed off. This woman's flesh was the same deep gold as the rocks of the cliff. She seemed to be part of the stone somehow, and she glowed softly, with her own golden light.

"A mortal!" she said, her voice husky and hesitant, as though not often used.

"I'm ever so sorry—" he began again.

"Hush!" the woman cautioned him sharply. She gestured to the folds of fur on her lap. It looked to be some kind of rug, but Devin moved closer and realized it was a lion's head resting on her knee. The huge creature attached to it was alive and snoring softly.

"The manticore?"

"Don't wake him up," the woman warned.

Devin had no intention of doing so. But he crept even closer to look at the beast, curiosity stronger than fear. The body was like a lion's; the enormous head was like a lion's, too, surrounded by a thick brown mane braided with beads and feathers. The face was a man's, although like the beast's body, it too was covered with tawny lion's fur. The monster looked peaceful, if you didn't know it had three rows of razor teeth. Its spiked and poisonous scorpion tail was draped around the golden woman.

"Are you a prisoner?" Devin asked.

"An oread," the woman corrected him.

"A nymph!" he exclaimed, remembering his studies in the *Basset*'s library. "A nymph who lives in caves and grottos. Cousin to dryads and nereids."

The nymph was pleased by this recognition. "You're an educated young man, I see. Not like so many mortals these days. You have come, I assume, to seek the door to the Faery Queen's realm?"

"I seek my sister," Devin explained. "Perhaps she passed this way last night? She looks a bit like me, only prettier and much more lively."

The woman stroked the massive head in her lap. "No one came this way last night. But there are other doors to the Realm. She may have passed through one of those."

"The Aisling family entered the Realm this way, years ago. Do you remember them?"

The oread shook her golden head. "That was when the Old One was here."

"The Old One?" Dev asked, puzzled.

"The old manticore. He went off with a sphinx, they say. So the faeries found a young manticore to come and guard the Realm for them. And I'm his nymph. I pet him, comb his mane, and share his cave."

"A young manticore," said Devin warily. "Is that more or less dangerous than the older kind?"

"Much more dangerous," the nymph said proudly. "He's very strong and fierce, and he loves to feast on human flesh. Fortunately, mine would taste like stone. Be on your way, mortal boy, before my man wakes up and finds you."

Devin needed no more encouragement. He followed the passage she pointed to and hurried on through the musk-scented cave, avoiding looking down at the litter of bones crunching underfoot.

Devin left the cave on the stream's other side. His clothes were damp from spray and mist, and he shivered. The sun had disappeared. The day had turned to dusk over here while on the other side of the stream the sun was still shining brightly.

The trail led him into a forest that seemed as old as time itself, full of hawthorn, holly, oak, and elder trees of massive size. Among the trees were the crumbling stones and marble walls of an ancient palace. Archways, columns, and doorways leading nowhere: all were covered with moss. Briar roses, thorns, and ivy climbed over marble statuary of mythical beasts, nymphs, and forgotten goddesses, tumbled and broken.

One of the statues was more intact than the others—a tall, beautiful white horse, so well carved it seemed to breathe as it peered through the ivy and thorns. The statue was so lifelike that Devin half expected the horse to move. Then it actually did, tossing the weeds aside to stand before the boy.

It wasn't a statue at all, it was a real horse—muscular and magnificent. It bowed to Devin in a peculiarly human fashion, then kneeled down in the moss, seeming to expect the boy to climb up on its broad white back.

"Have you come from Titania's court?" asked Devin.

The handsome head bobbed up and down, and the boy let out a grateful breath. If the faery court had sent the horse, then Gwen must be there already.

Devin climbed onto the creature's back. The horse rose gracefully, then suddenly reared on its hind legs and raced off through the trees. Devin felt a surge of fear, for the horse was faster than any he'd known. The trees were soon a blur of motion, branches whipping his arms and face. He ducked his head, grabbed handfuls of white mane, and hung on for dear life.

The horse kept going faster and faster, sailing over streams, boulders, and the scattered ruins of old stone walls. It bounded through sharp thorns and thickets, leapt the bracken, crashed through the briars. "Stop! Stop!" Devin cried. It would kill him before they reached the court.

The horse stopped with a suddenness that sent Devin flying over its neck. He landed in a squishy bog, the blow softened by water and mud. The horse reared over him and *laughed*. It was a strangely human sound. Then it spun on its hooves and leapt away, vanishing into the trees.

Devin closed his eyes as he lay in the mud. He was winded and bruised, his pack was gone, his clothes were torn, and his head pounded. He hadn't the foggiest notion of where he was—or where his sister might be. For the first time since he'd set foot on the *Basset,* he gave in to despair.

He lay there for a long while, aching, his eyes squeezed shut, fighting back tears—till he felt something wet and cold on his cheek. Devin shivered and opened his eyes. A small brown weasel sat near his left shoulder, quietly watching him. Its little nose was pressed against his cheek. Its eyes were green.

"Hullo, little one," Devin said weakly. "You must be wondering what I'm doing here. Well, so am I." He put out a scratched, muddy hand for the weasel to sniff, then he stroked its fur.

"I don't know what I'm going to do now," he confided to the furry brown creature. "I need to find Queen Titania, and I've no idea where she is."

The weasel opened its little pink mouth. "I'll take you to the Queen."

The air shimmered, and the weasel became a girl with eyes as green as grass. She was almost as tall as Devin, and pelted all over with soft brown fur.

"What *are* you?" he asked in wonder.

"A faery, of course," she replied cheerfully. "Did you think we all had butterfly wings?"

"No," he answered honestly, "but I wasn't expecting whiskers and fur."

"I'm a guardian faery," the girl explained. "I look after the little ones of the woods. Other faeries look after the flowers, the fishes, the snakes and bugs—oh, all kinds of things. What kind of a creature are you? Are you a Mortal?" She sniffed. "You smell like one."

"My name is Devin," he told the girl. "I came on the *Basset,* from a place called Cornwall."

"Cornwall!" the faery squealed, delighted. "That's where my tribe comes from too! My mama's a piskie. That's a Cornish faery. Do you know my Cornish cousins, Dev-vin?"

"You're the first faery I've ever seen in my life," Devn admitted.

"You've never seen faeries before? How awful for you!" The girl gave him a pitying look. "Don't worry. You'll see all sorts of faeries at Queen Titania's court."

"Can you really take me there?" he asked quickly.

The faery promptly picked him up in her arms, as though he were just a small child.

Dev blinked in surprise. She seemed like such a delicate girl, slender and pretty, yet now she carried him out of the bog as if he weighed nothing at all. She climbed a mossy bank, passed between two rowan trees, then set him down.

"Look," she said, pointing at a clearing of emerald green grass ahead. "The Lady you seek is just over there."

"We're here already?" Devin was startled. "I had no idea we were so close."

The weasel faery cocked her head and looked at him, reminding Devin of Gwen's "bird look." "It was a short distance for me," she explained. "For you, it could have taken a lifetime."

"Then I'm grateful to you," he said humbly. "So where, er, is Titania exactly?"

"Why, right there, with her court, of course!"

"That field looks empty to me," he admitted.

"Well, close your eyes and look again," she told him patiently.

Devin did as the weasel faery instructed. He closed his eyes, took a deep breath, opened them—and the scene had changed. Now the clearing held bright tent pavilions, a busy outdoor marketplace, a drilling ground, where faery knights were practicing with swords and shields, and faeries of every description strolling on the ground and swooping through the sky. It looked like one of his father's big paintings about King Arthur's court. But *these* knights had long silver hair, and green armor, and faery wings. Their swords were made of sparkling light, and the cloth of their tent pavilions shimmered with every color of the rainbow—including colors he'd never seen before.

"Come, Dev-vin," said the weasel faery, taking him firmly by the hand. She strode briskly into the clearing, between tents and through the crowds.

He tried hard not to stare as they passed—although all the faeries were staring at him, stopping what they were doing to stand and gape at the human boy. He saw now that the books were right—*all* of them, with their contrary opinions. The faeries were tiny *and* tall, gentle-looking *and* fierce. Some flew on wings made of color and light; others had wings like birds or bats. Still others had no wings at all and seemed to be made of clumps of earth, with moss and leaves for hair, clothes made of bark, and sticklike limbs. They crowded around the boy as he passed, reaching out long faery fingers to stroke his cheek and touch his hair. He heard whispers and giggling. "What is it?" he heard. "A human!" "A boy!" "A mortal!" "A creature with eyes brown as mud!" He seemed to be as marvelous to them as they were to him.

The weasel faery ignored them, her nose in the air, looking proud despite the tattered dress she wore and the mud on her pelted feet. She led him straight across the clearing to the largest pavilion of all, made with acres of pure white cloth, hung with banners and silver bells.

The faeries around this tent were the loveliest creatures Devin had ever seen. The women wore pale gossamer dresses that fluttered softly in the breeze and shimmered like the light of a star—or Cassandra Aisling's pendant. They were tall and slender, with rippling hair, just like the women in Papa's paintings. (And Devin began to wonder if Papa had been to this court himself.) The faery men were as splendid as their women, with flashing eyes and long braided hair. They wore golden bands at wrist and throat, and jewels upon their fingers.

This was all Devin had time to observe as his friend marched up to a tall faery knight. "Human boy," the weasel faery explained. "He's come to see the Queen." Then the girl bowed, turned her head to wink at Devin, and vanished into the crowd.

The faery knight looked Devin up and down, yet his words were welcoming. He said, "The Queen has been expecting you. I'll take you to her, boy."

Devin's knees went weak with relief. If he was expected, then Gwen must be here. He followed the knight into the tent, searching for a glimpse of his twin and completely oblivious to his own muddy and bedraggled state. Throughout the pavilion, faeries of astonishing beauty lounged on rugs and golden pillows, talking, laughing, playing chess with figures of delicate blown glass. An odd trio of beak-nosed faeries played music on carved wooden harps, a few maidens danced, and a feast was served by tiny creatures with huge silver trays. The courtiers stared at the human child with frank curiosity. The faery knight looked back and grinned, which gave Devin fresh courage.

Devin made his way through the faery lords and ladies at the center of the tent. He heard the faery knight announce, "The human child has come, my lords."

Where were Titania and Oberon? He couldn't find them in the throng. Then the knight took his wrist and drew Dev forward, presenting him to the Queen.

There was no throne, just a low dais covered with green velvet and leaves. Titania sat with her skirts draped around her, stars bright in her silver hair. A white dove perched on the Queen's left knee. Another fed on seeds from her palm. Oberon sat beside her, his face as ageless and as beautiful as hers. He smiled as Devin bowed deeply, but she was the one who spoke.

"Rise, child. Come sit with us. It gladdens my heart to see you here."

"You knew I was coming, then," Devin said.

But before the boy could ask about Gwen, the knight instructed him to sit. He perched at the edge of the dais at Titania's feet as she explained. "The doves brought me a message from Cassandra Aisling in the World Outside. So we knew a child would come to us soon, bearing a portrait of our friends. Then, last night, my doves brought other news: they said a mortal child had fallen into the Dark Queen's hands. We are much relieved that this news is wrong and you've made it safely through the woods. We hope you've kept the portrait safe as well." Her eyes were questioning.

Devin looked up at the dazzling faery. "I don't know who the Dark Queen is. But I'm not the one who carried the portrait. My sister, Gwen, has the Aislings' painting. She's here with you, isn't she?"

A look passed between the Queen and the King. Oberon spoke, his expression troubled. "We do not know this 'Gwen' you speak of. You are the only mortal here. You say it's your sister who carries the painting? Not you? Where is she now?"

"I thought she was here, with you," said Devin. "If she's not, then I don't know where she is!"

"Perhaps she's the one," Titania said to her husband.

"The one what?" Devin demanded loudly, too worried about his sister to remain in awe of royalty.

Titania's voice was gentle when she spoke, but her words fell heavy as stones nonetheless. "We fear she's the one who's been taken under the hill by the Raven Queen."

"But who is this Raven Queen?" said the boy. "What would she want with my sister Gwen?"

"Nicnevin is my dark twin," the Faery Queen explained. "She rules the night as I rule the day. She rules that part of Faery you mortals call the Unseelie Court. While all you see here is the Seelie Court, which is in my charge."

These were names Devin recognized. He'd read about the Unseelie Court in the library on the *Basset*. They were dangerous faeries who had no love of man or anything mortal.

"And that's the court my sister has gone to?" Devin asked the Queen, appalled.

The King said, "That is what we fear."

"Then we have to get her out of there!" Devin exclaimed, jumping to his feet.

Titania met his gaze with her own. He could see the sorrow in her ageless eyes, but also a monarch's firm resolve. She was a queen, the ruler of this realm, and her first concerns were not mortal concerns. "I'm sorry, child. But I cannot help you. I cannnot risk full war with the Unseelie Court to save one mortal girl. It would be useless. No one ever returns from under the hill."

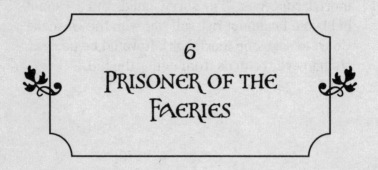

6
Prisoner of the Faeries

For a long time after Thomas left her room, Gwen couldn't move from the bed. She sat there stunned, trying to make sense of what he had told her. *Thomas must have exaggerated,* she finally comforted herself. *He's a storyteller, after all.*

Gwen simply couldn't accept that she would be trapped under the hill forever. There had to be a way out. King Arthur's knight Sir Gawain had gotten himself out of a magical bargain in which he was supposed to get his head chopped off—simply by being brave.

So I shall be very brave, she resolved.

Her door suddenly flew open, and the violet faery flew in. She buzzed around the room, rather like a large purple mosquito. "Still in bed, lazy girl?"

"I am not lazy," Gwen informed her.

"Well, then get up," Violet Faery snapped. "The Queen has summoned you."

"The Queen," Gwen repeated carefully. "Do you mean Titania?"

Crystalline laughter filled the small room. "How should I know what Titania does or wants?" the violet faery asked. She flew to the top of the table and perched on its edge. "I serve my lady, Queen Nicnevin."

Gwen got out of bed and stalked toward the desk. "You tricked me," she said angrily.

"Only because you were so easy to trick," the faery assured her, darting to the top of the wardrobe. "I couldn't resist. Now, stop standing around with your mouth hanging open, and get dressed."

Gwen looked for her dress. She'd dropped it on the chair before going to sleep. But the beautiful azure blue dress was no longer there. She opened the wardrobe and saw only a shapeless dull brown shift.

Gwen's heart began to hammer. The jeweled dress couldn't be gone! Not the dress with Mama's painting sewn into the skirt!

She forced herself to speak calmly. It wouldn't do to let the violet faery know how worried she was. "Last night I left my dress on the chair. It's no longer here."

The faery carelessly waved a delicate hand. "Why do you want to wear that filthy thing? You ought to be grateful we took it from your room to clean it. Wear the dress we left you."

Gwen held up the brown shapeless shift. "This? I've seen better-looking potato sacks!"

"Beggars can't be choosers," the faery told her with her feral smile. Then the smile disappeared, and her eyes flashed furious purple sparks. "Now, get dressed, and don't make me tell you again!"

Sullenly, Gwen did as she was told. Then she followed Violet Faery back through the narrow tunnels to the throne room. The throne room looked much as it had the night before. The air was a dusk gray that even the torchlight couldn't fully brighten.

Thomas once again stood in the line of the Queen's courtiers, his expression as deliberately blank as before, even when the violet faery buzzed around his head and hovered near his ear. Gwen was sure she was insulting him.

Even though she knew she shouldn't let on that they'd talked, Gwen sent Thomas a sympathetic look. It was hard *not* to look at him. He was beautiful, he was her only friend here, and he seemed even more gaunt than he had before.

Nicnevin sat on her throne, her golden eyes glittering. "Ah, it's my young guest," she said.

"Did you sleep well last night, Gwenevere?"

"Reasonably," Gwen replied. Her mind was whirring. How should one behave when addressing the Queen of the Unseelie Court?

"And did you find everything you needed?" Nicnevin asked. She sounded as though she were the concierge of a fine hotel, inquiring after a guest.

"My dress disappeared while I slept," Gwen said honestly.

The Raven Queen favored her with a feral smile. "Of course. I gave orders that it was to be cleaned."

"And," Gwen grew bolder, "I asked for paints and found only a pen, ink, and paper."

One of Nicnevin's black brows rose. "Do you mean to tell me you're the sort of artist who is only capable of working in paint? You don't know how to draw—is that it?"

"No," Gwen said, stung. "Of course I can draw. I've drawn ever since I was old enough to hold a pencil." She suddenly had a brilliant idea—she could bargain with her art! She would draw an absolutely gorgeous portrait of the Dark Queen, and Nicnevin would be so grateful that she would release Gwen and Thomas from her magical hold and maybe even give them fabulous faery gifts.

"If you'll give me a piece of charcoal and a

sheet of paper," Gwen proposed, "I'll draw you now, sitting there on your throne."

"You're quite demanding for a captive," Nicnevin observed, but as she spoke a raven dropped a stick of charcoal at Gwen's feet, and another, a sheet of creamy white paper.

"Thank you," Gwen said.

She had no proper easel or drawing table, so she flattened the paper against one of the silver floor tiles. She cocked her head and closed one eye—it helped her to sharpen her focus and see more clearly. *If Dev were here, he'd tease me about my "bird eye,"* she thought with a pang. Who would have ever guessed?—she was actually missing her twin.

The Raven Queen sat perfectly still, her black hair gleaming in the torchlight. Gwen couldn't help wondering if she'd sat for portraits before. For a long moment, Gwen studied Nicnevin— noting the line of her throat, the curve of her cheekbones, the slant of her eyes—then she tossed back her own dark hair and began to draw.

Gwen was still working on Nicnevin's face when she became aware that someone was peering over her shoulder—a small green faery with a lemon-shaped head, blue wings, and a curious expression on his face. Gwen couldn't help smiling at him. "Haven't you ever seen anyone draw before?" she asked.

He shook his head.

"Well, I'll show it to you when I'm done," she promised, "but it's hard for me to draw with someone peering over my shoulder."

"Mugwort, come here," Nicnevin suddenly ordered.

Gwen was surprised to see the green faery trembling as he flew toward his queen. Nicnevin patted her knee, and he lit there, trembling all the harder.

The Queen patted his head, then with one hand on his head and the other on his collarbone, and—without a second's hesitation—she snapped his neck.

"Wh-what have you done?" Gwen stammered. "He—he wasn't causing any trouble. He only wanted to see what I was doing."

"I did not give him leave to do so," Nicnevin said. Carelessly, she tossed Mugwort's limp form to the floor. Gwen stared in horrified disbelief as Nicnevin waved a hand and her ravens flew down from the golden columns and began to tear at the little faery's body.

Gwen covered her eyes and fought back tears. She was more frightened than she'd ever been. She knew now that everything Thomas had said was true. He hadn't exaggerated. If anything, he hadn't told her the half of it.

Nicnevin's rich voice floated through the hall.

"I suppose I can see *some* resemblance," she said thoughtfully, "but it's really quite crude."

Gwen opened her eyes to see that the Faery Queen was holding her portrait. Her horrid ravens must have brought it to her.

"The drawing isn't finished," Gwen protested. "I've only just begun!"

The Dark Queen gave her a gracious smile. "Well, there's really no point in going on, is there? You have so little talent. And I have other duties to attend to—as do you. Violet Faery, give the poor girl work that she's capable of performing."

"B-but—" Gwen sputtered, ignoring a frantic look from Thomas.

"Are you questioning me, mortal?" A dangerous edge came into the Raven Queen's voice.

"I was just wondering," Gwen explained quickly.

"In my realm, you do not wonder," Nicnevin told her. "You obey." She glanced meaningfully at the remains of poor Mugwort. "Do you understand me, child?"

"Yes," Gwen said, her voice a whisper. "I understand."

She meant to obey. She was almost out of the throne room when she saw her—a pretty faery girl with red-gold hair, who was wearing the blue jeweled dress. *Her* blue dress. The mud stains

were gone, and Gwen could only wonder if
Mama's painting was still safe inside. She forgot
about following the violet faery and started
toward the dress.

"Ouch!" Gwen cried as Violet Faery's sharp
little teeth sank into her shoulder.

"Stupid girl! Do you *want* the ravens after
you?"

Gwen, for once, knew better than to answer
back. She took a last look at her beloved dress
and followed Violet Faery out.

Again, Gwen was led through narrow, winding
tunnels, but also through an enclosed courtyard
whose walls were lined with porcelain urns.
Bright blue vines trailed from each of the
planters. They were pretty, Gwen thought, but
also disturbing; no normal vine would be that
color. The courtyard led to a cavelike room, a
conservatory that was filled with a great many
aromatic plants sprouting blood red flowers. The
conservatory led to an elegant parlor, which in
turn led to a music room, filled with instruments
of every description—harps and drums and fid-
dles and flutes. The music room opened into a
long faery-thronged gallery, which in turn led to
a formal banquet room nearly as large as the
throne room. A narrow stairway connected the
banquet room to a kitchen.

Finally, the violet faery opened a door at the very back of the kitchen—and shoved Gwen into an enormous scullery. While the other rooms of the faery palace had been spotlessly clean, the scullery was a mess. Pots and pans and plates and goblets were stacked on every surface. The dishes were piled so thick and high that Gwen couldn't see the counters or tables or shelves beneath them.

Violet Faery handed her an apron and a sponge the size of a shilling.

"What are these for?" Gwen asked.

"For cleaning, of course," the faery told her. She waved toward a particularly odious pile of pots. "I believe you'll find a basin of water under there. And"—she handed Gwen a thin, dirt-encrusted bar of soap—"you'll need this."

"You can't be serious!" Gwen exclaimed. "I'm an artist, not a servant."

"Nicnevin doesn't think much of your talents," the faery reminded her, and Gwen found herself blinking back tears of hurt. No one had ever been so cruel about her art. Papa had even said to her once, "You must not let on to your siblings, but you are the most talented of the lot. You've got a rare gift, Gwen. You were born with an artist's eye and an artist's hands. If you work hard, everything you create will have beauty in it."

Gwenevere lifted her head proudly. "Nicnevin may think what she likes," she told Violet Faery. "Nevertheless, I don't scrub dishes. It's not what I was born for."

Violet Faery smiled and pointed to a shelf near the ceiling. A large raven perched there, watching her every move. "Do you want him to tell Nicnevin that you refuse her will?" the faery asked.

"No," Gwen said quickly.

"I didn't think so. Make sure that after you clean all the dirty dishes, you scrub the counters and the shelves and the floor." The faery's sharp teeth gleamed. "You would not want the Lady to find fault with your work."

Gwen was too angry to answer. She took the tiny sponge and the even tinier piece of soap and went in search of the water basin.

"I'll return for you later," Violet Faery promised as she flew out the door. The raven remained.

"Stop staring at me," Gwen told the bird, but she started to work.

The search for the water basin was a disgusting one. The dishes were caked and crusted with food, the pans sticky with sauces. Gwen shuddered as she picked up a goblet filled with green furry mold. Her stomach churned. Everything looked foul and smelled worse.

Tears rolled from Gwen's eyes as she worked. How had her wonderful, magical adventure turned into such a disaster? Was she really to spend the rest of her days scrubbing the faeries' filthy pots? Would she never see her home or her family again? She wondered what had become of her brother, and rubbed tears from her eyes. At least Devin wasn't Nicnevin's prisoner.

Gwen never knew how many hours she worked. But in the time that she was left in the scullery, she felt as though she aged. Her back ached and her feet hurt, and she developed a new appreciation for the Thornworths' servants. It suddenly occurred to her that they worked very hard indeed, and that it must be dreary to spend your entire life cleaning up after others. Her life in Cornwall and London suddenly seemed a tremendously privileged one. She'd never once had to wash a glass or even pick up after herself. She'd always known that someone else would take care of whatever mess she left.

Whenever Gwen stopped to stretch her back or take a rest, the raven would swoop down and begin shrieking and pulling at her hair—until Gwen didn't even let herself think about resting. Though every muscle in her body ached with exhaustion, she scrubbed and rinsed and scrubbed some more.

Gwen had just started to scour a filthy copper cauldron when the violet faery returned. "You're not done?" she demanded. "Have you been twiddling your thumbs all this time?"

"I have done nothing but work," Gwen replied through gritted teeth.

"You're not only lazy, you're a liar," the faery scolded. "You haven't cleaned a quarter of the dishes here. And you've not started on the floor or the counters or—"

"Ask him!" Gwen said, scowling at the raven.

The faery did, in fact, fly up to the raven's perch, and they seemed to converse for quite some time.

The violet faery fluttered down to Gwen. "He says you speak the truth," she reported. "So you will be allowed to return to your room for the night. You will be brought back here in the morning to finish."

"Oh, lovely!" Gwen muttered, but not too loudly.

She followed the violet faery back through the kitchen and banquet hall and gallery and music room and parlor. In the conservatory, she noticed that all the flowers had been cut. And when they reached the great courtyard, she understood why.

The courtyard was filled with Nicnevin's courtiers, all of them mounted on horses.

Though she was no longer quite so enamored of faeries, even Gwen had to admit they were a marvel to behold. There were tiny, delicate horses for the smallest faeries and large, powerful chargers for Nicnevin's attendants, and the blood red flowers from the conservatory were wound through every mane and tail. The faeries themselves wore dark chain mail that glittered as though it were woven from marcasite. Red banners hung from their lances, and a raven was engraved on each shield. Restlessly, the horses and their riders wheeled about, trotting back and forth in the confined space.

"What is this?" Gwen asked the violet faery.

"I thought you'd know. They're going out on a Faery Rade—when the Faery Host rides abroad and takes what it wants from your kind."

Gwen bit her lip. She'd heard of Faery Rades, of course. Papa had even painted one. But Papa's Rade had been a glorious cavalcade—a procession of the most beautiful and magical beings beneath a luminous moon. This Rade had an altogether different feel. It made her think of the time she'd walked past an arena in London where a boxing match was to be held. Men had crowded the street outside, eager for the ticket office to open. Now, the Unseelie Court had that same air—everyone milling about, thirsting for the blood that would be spilled.

A green-skinned faery girl on a dappled steed trotted by and smiled that awful feral smile at Gwen. Beneath glittering armor, the girl wore Gwen's azure blue dress.

"Wait!" Gwen started after the girl. "Please! That's my dress and—"

She stopped as a tall, night black stallion stepped directly in front of her. Nicnevin sat astride it, dressed in blood red armor. A raven rode on her shoulder, another on her wrist.

"Gwenevere." The Faery Queen's golden eyes seemed to bore right through her, and Gwen felt her throat go dry with fear. "Nothing here is yours unless I give it to you."

Without another glance at the girl, the Raven Queen called to her troops, and the Unseelie Court rode from the courtyard with a great jingling of bridles and a clattering of hooves, passing beneath a stone archway that Gwen had not seen before.

"Does that lead to the crystal door?" Gwen wondered aloud. Surely, the horses would not attempt that endless, winding stairway.

Violet Faery pinched her hard. "Any part of the hill can lead to the crystal door if we will it. Now, back to your room, foolish girl."

In her room, Gwen found a bowl of what smelled like a delicious beef stew. She debated a moment. She hadn't eaten since the night before, and her stomach was growling. Besides, she'd already eaten their food. *It can't make anything worse,* she reasoned.

She ate three spoonfuls of the stew, then pushed it away in disgust. It had no flavor at all. And she did feel worse. Her mind now raced with an endless list of all the things that had gone wrong. She was a talentless captive who would spend the rest of her life scrubbing a filthy scullery. She'd lost Mama's painting—it was probably out on some Faery Rade at this very minute. That was, *if* the painting was still in the azure blue dress. What if the faeries had discovered it? Gwen couldn't bear to think of her mother's work in the hands of the Unseelie Court.

She winced as she thought about that morning—her grand, proud scheme to draw Nicnevin and win freedom for herself and Thomas. Had anyone ever been more deluded?

Then Gwen's thoughts circled to the one thing she hadn't let herself think about. The faery named Mugwort. He was part of the Unseelie Court and probably as unpleasant as the rest, but Gwen couldn't help remembering the look of wonder in his eyes as he'd watched her draw. And he had lost his life because of her. Because of her ridiculous, impractical plan!

Gwen put her head down on the table and

wept. Nothing in her life had ever been this bad. For once, her imagination failed her. She couldn't imagine that any of this would ever get better.

The door to her room inched open, and Gwen wiped her eyes. No matter what, she would never let Violet Faery see her in tears. But it was Thomas who entered, leaning on a walking staff. The little mouse peeked out of his shirt pocket, and Gwen noted that the mouse looked far more robust than the Rhymer.

"What's wrong?" she asked. "Did you hurt your leg?"

Thomas shook his head impatiently. "No, I'm just a little shaky." He held up the stick. "I cut down a broom to fashion this. Do you think Nic-nevin will notice?"

"She probably already has," Gwen said. "I think she notices everything—she or one of her horrid ravens."

Thomas shrugged. "I'm a dying man, anyway. What I can't figure out is why she keeps me around."

"Probably for her own amusement. She's so cruel, she probably takes pleasure in watching you waste away."

"That's as good a guess as any." Thomas sat on the edge of the bed, and Gwen saw that he'd grown so thin his skin was almost translucent. "How are you holding up, young Gwen?"

"Hating myself," she answered honestly. She stood and faced him. "I—I thought I was going to set us free," she explained. "This morning when I offered to draw Nicnevin, I thought she would be pleased with my portrait and grant us our freedom. Instead, my brilliant plan cost poor Mugwort his life."

"If it wasn't you, Nicnevin would have found some other excuse to kill."

"That doesn't make it any better!" Gwen covered her face as the tears began again. "He was so little and curious—if it hadn't been for me—"

Without a word, Thomas got to his feet and folded her into his arms. He swayed a bit in the effort to keep himself upright, but he held her gently until she had no more tears to cry.

"I'm sorry," she sniffed, embarrassed for having thoroughly soaked the front of his shirt.

"Don't be sorry for tears," he said with a smile. "The faeries never cry, you know. That you can is proof that you're mortal and that you have a heart—both of which I find to be a great comfort in this place."

"I—I just get so scared. And I miss everything," Gwen confessed. "My home, my family, my sister Elaine's demented parrot. Even my practical brother—especially him," she added with another sniff.

"I miss the sun," Thomas said. "And the rain.

The colors of the sky when the dawn is breaking, walking the coast in a storm, eating warm bread with sweet honey. I spent my days pining to find the Faery Realm, and now that I've found it, the simple pleasures of Earth seem to me a paradise lost."

Gwen swallowed hard. "We're really never going to see any of that again, are we?"

Thomas's dark eyes held hers. "Probably not. So it seems to me the best we can do is not to forget it. Let me tell you a story…Once, many years ago, there lived a brother and sister. As it happens, their mother died and their stepmother was cruel. She beat them and gave them only crusts of bread to eat, so the brother said to the sister, 'Let us go away from this place and into the wide world.'"

Gwen sat down on the floor, leaning against the bed (it was the most comfortable spot in the room), and gave herself up to the Rhymer's story. His voice was soothing, and it was a comfort to think about the plight of someone else.

"So they set out without food or water—for their stepmother would have noticed if they'd taken any. They walked over hills and fields, and finally, as darkness fell, they entered a vast forest. Unlike some people"—Thomas winked at her—"they had the sense not to go plunging into the dark wood. They made camp and fell asleep.

They were so tired and weakened by hunger that they slept until the sun was high. The brother woke first. 'I'm thirsty,' he said to his sister. 'But I hear a stream nearby. Let's find it and drink—'"

Thomas stopped speaking as the mouse in his pocket began frantically squeaking. "Someone may be coming," he told Gwen.

"Probably that wretched violet faery," Gwen said.

"I don't think she's so bad," Thomas said to her surprise. "Still, it won't do for me to be caught in here. I'd better go."

"Of course, but...what happens to the brother and sister? You have to tell me the end of the story."

Thomas sighed. "Well, the short version is that the brother finds three streams, and each one warns him not to drink, but he's so thirsty that he drinks anyway and is turned into a stag."

"Oh." This was not the ending Gwen wanted to hear.

"And eventually—after a great many more adventures—he and his sister make it out of the forest, and he's returned to his human form."

"That's better," she said, relieved. "I didn't want it to end without a bit of hope."

"There's always a bit of hope," Thomas told her as he reached for the door. "And, Gwen, don't believe what Nicnevin said about your art. She was trying to make you doubt yourself—I think that may be one of her greatest talents."

Gwen smiled. "Good night, Thomas."

She climbed into the lumpy bed, thinking about the Rhymer's story. She pictured the brother and sister, so hungry and thirsty and lost. And she pictured Thomas, wasting away before her eyes. It hurt to see that he now needed a staff to walk. How much longer before he couldn't walk at all?

And then Gwen had an idea. Perhaps she couldn't save herself. But there might be a way— a very practical way—to at least keep Thomas alive. She just prayed she could make it work before it was too late.

7
JOURNEY TO
THE DARK REALM

Devin walked through the faery encampment in an angry daze. Titania had refused to help! His sister was the prisoner of Nicnevin, the Raven Queen, and nobody seemed to care.

He crossed the crowded marketplace, barely watching where he stepped. Little hands reached out to stroke his hair and cheeks. He swatted them all away. The faeries saw his scowling face, backed off, and let him pass.

A heavy hand fell on Devin's shoulder. He whirled around, his own hand raised in a fist— then dropped his arm, embarrassed, when he saw it was the King.

"Come. Walk with me," said Oberon.

Devin nodded silently. He let Oberon lead him out of the clearing and into the shadowed trees. They followed no trail Devin could see, but presently, by twists and turns, they came upon a lonely lake surrounded by thick woodland. The dusky air seemed heavier here. In the distance were those swirling lights that looked like fireflies but that Devin now knew to be tiny faeries. Oberon sat on smooth black stone that tumbled down to the water's edge. Devin did likewise, dangling his feet above the still water.

"You mustn't think the Queen is hard and cruel," Oberon said to the boy. "She'd save your sister if she could. She'd storm the hill with a troop of knights! But her first concern is the Seelie Court—and if we go to war, lives will be lost. Think what a tragedy that is for creatures otherwise immortal."

Think what a tragedy it is to lose your sister, Devin wanted to snap. But he said nothing. The Queen was only being sensible, after all. *Sensible.* He hated that word right now. And this whole island.

"I don't understand," the boy said, emotion thick in his husky voice, "why saving my sister is bound to start a war with the Unseelie Court."

"The Raven Queen will use any excuse. She delights in war, and holds life cheap. To keep the truce, we are bound by its terms—we must not interfere in her affairs, and she, in turn, stays out of ours. You're safe here in the Seelie realm. Your sister would have been safe too had she not gone into those woods at night, the Dark Queen's time."

"What does Nicnevin want with Gwen?"

"She is no friend of mortals, child. Not all faeries are good, or to be trusted—didn't you know that? The Unseelie Court makes storms at sea, steals small babies from their beds, blights the crops of farmers, and causes harm to all who cross them. Mortals befriended by the Seelie Court earn their particular dislike."

"Does that mean I'm in danger from them, too? Because I'm here with you?"

"They may not know about you, unless your sister has said something. But the Aislings are certainly in danger now, because of the painting."

"I don't see why," Dev commented, throwing a stone into the lake. It disappeared, leaving only lazy circles of ripples behind it.

"Tell me," said the Faery King, "did Miranda pose in a long white dress? Did Cassandra wear a stone pendant? These were gifts from us. The Raven Queen is sure to recognize them."

The boy frowned thoughtfully. A plan was forming in his mind—a way to bargain with the Seelie Court to aid Gwen's escape.

"The painting might be safe," he said. Oberon turned and looked at him while Devin explained how the painting came to be sewn into his sister's dress. "Gwen is very bright, you know. She wouldn't have handed that portrait over to the wrong faery queen."

"You think not?" Oberon said eagerly. "You think she's kept it hidden away?"

"I'm almost certain of it," Devin insisted. He glanced shrewdly at the King. "But we have to get Gwen *and* the dress out of the hill before it's found."

The Faery King held Devin's gaze, his ageless eyes grown wide and dark. "There's no need to bargain with me, child. I'll gladly give you what help I can, for your sake, and your sister's, and not just for the Aisling girls. The Queen and I have talked of nothing else over the last few hours."

Devin stared at the faery lord. "Then why did she say you would not help?" Confusion and profound relief were clear upon his face.

"The Queen cannot be seen to help your quest in an official way. Nor can our army help you—we have no power under the hill. But you, child—you're mortal. You can get into Nicnevin's hall. And when you're there, you must use your wits and bargain for your sister's life."

"I'll do anything," Devin said gravely. "But what have *I* got to bargain with?"

"Ah," said the King, a gleam in his eye, "I've come up with a plan."

Oberon explained his plan at length and

Devin listened carefully, asking questions, taking notes in his methodical, sensible way. He meant exactly what he'd said: he'd do anything to rescue Gwen. But no one left the Raven Queen's hall, and the odds were stacked against them.

"...So if I go disguised as a harper, you're certain the Unseelie Court will let me in?" Devin asked.

"Not just any harper," Oberon explained, "but the greatest harper of all. The Unseelie Court won't dare turn Thomas the Rhymer from their door. Their Queen is fond of harp music, and Thomas the Rhymer is a prize. She's never seen the man, and she won't know that you're not him."

"There's just one thing," Devin interrupted. "I don't sing, or play the harp. What do I do if she actually calls upon me to perform?"

Oberon smiled cannily. "I intend to place a spell on you. You'll have great skill—for a limited time. When you carry the harp before the Unseelie Court, you'll play perfectly."

Devin swallowed. The thought of performing before a crowd made his stomach hurt. Gwenevere was the actress of the family, not him. He stammered and fumbled his lines. Yet this time he'd be under a spell, and that would give him confidence, surely. *This is for Gwen,* he reminded himself. "All right," he said, "I'll do it."

"You'll need a guide," said Oberon. "There's one who travels between the realms, at home in both the dark and the light. He's agreed to guide you to the hall. I'll summon him now."

The King spoke a word in a strange language, and a light appeared at his fingertips. The light flew off into the trees, and then, shortly, it reappeared. This time, a creature followed, a faery shaped like a man above the waist and like a goat below. One leg was covered with black goat fur, the other leg was covered with white. Two horns curved over his head. He kneeled before King Oberon.

"You called for me, Lord?" His tone was respectful, but the look in his eyes was wild and sly. There was something familiar about him, and Devin found himself backing up a pace.

"Pooka, this is Devin Thornworth. The mortal boy we've spoken of."

"We've met," said the pooka. Then he laughed, and Devin knew who the creature was.

"You were that wicked white horse!" he cried. "The one who threw me in a bog!"

"Wicked?" The pooka was indignant. "I merely played a good trick on you. It was very funny. Wasn't it funny? Wasn't it a good trick, Devinthornworth?"

"Pooka," Oberon said sternly, "there will be no more tricks from you now. Mortals are fragile.

They damage more easily than faeries."

The pooka hung his handsome head, but his golden eyes still gleamed. Devin didn't think he was sorry. And *this* was to be his guide?

"Pooka lives on the border," the King explained, "between the night and the day, able to cross between the two. Any other faery from our court would raise Nicnevin's suspicions. But Pooka is welcome in her hall, just as he is welcome here."

Devin didn't find this a comforting recommendation. If Pooka was welcome under the hill, how did they know he didn't serve the Raven Queen? He eyed the pooka warily. The creature grinned back, with horsey white teeth. "All right," Devin said reluctantly, "as long he's not a horse again."

"I can also be a big black dog," the pooka boasted, "with flame red eyes."

"Just be a man," Oberon suggested, "or as much of one as you can be. And if you betray this boy, I'll banish you from the Seelie Court."

"No tricks," said Pooka, hand on heart. He bowed again before the King.

Then he bounded away into the woods. Devin could hear him laughing.

The boy scowled at the clothes the faeries had given to him. He looked perfectly ridiculous, in velvet leggings, a green wool cape, a poet's shirt edged in lace, boots tied round with thongs of leather, and a harp upon his back. Gwen always tried to get him to dress like this. His face softened, thinking of her. If he could only get her out from under the hill, he'd wear whatever she wanted.

Pooka was pacing, eager to go. His eyes had a shifty gleam to them. He refused to help carry anything, so in addition to the harp, Devin carried his pack (rescued from a bramble patch) and a willow bag filled with food suitable for humankind. He took his leave of the King and Queen. No word was spoken of Nicnevin. Publicly, their plan did not exist, and the Seelie Court knew nothing of it. Yet Titania slipped a ring onto his finger and whispered, "For luck."

Devin followed the pooka into the ferny undergrowth of the faery woods. The pooka strode ahead, his white side flashing through the trees. The boy was glad to fall behind. He didn't relish such company. But he stayed alert—in case the pooka thought it would be *funny* to disappear.

They traveled this way throughout the day. The pooka never stopped for rest. Perhaps the creature didn't get hungry and tired as mortals do. It was hard to tell how much time passed, for an eerie mist blocked out the sun, muffling all sound and swirling ghostlike through the trees. After what seemed like hours, they reached what had once been a road, its cobblestones now carpeted with moss and wildflowers. They followed this through beech and birch, then cut through untracked woods once more. Soon they came to the weed-choked banks of a slow, meandering river. The water was shallow, passable, but it was colored a deep blood red. Devin looked at it warily.

The pooka grinned. "I'll carry you."

"Uh, no thank you," he said quickly.

The pooka shrugged and scratched at fleas. "There's a bridge down there, Devinthornworth. Myself, I like wet feet."

The boy followed the riverbank and found a most peculiar bridge, made of sticks and twigs that couldn't possibly hold his weight. He looked to the other riverbank. The pooka had already gone ahead. *"Credendo vides,"* he muttered to himself and stepped onto the bridge. It dipped and swayed, but it held him up. It trembled with every step he took. Yet he carried on, and soon he reached dry land on the other side.

Here, the dusk was deepening, and true darkness would soon descend. The night belonged to Nicnevin. Devin shivered in the gloaming.

"Wait," he called to his aggravating guide. The pooka trotted back. "We're entering her realm, aren't we? That river marks the border."

The pooka grinned, baring his horsey teeth. "You're right. Now, let's go on."

"Well, I'm not an immortal, see? I need a rest. I need to eat. And I want you to wait for me." Devin turned his back on the pooka.

He busily took off harp and pack, wondering what the pooka would do now. He half expected the creature to shrug and leave him in the darkening woods, but when he turned, the pooka had started a fire from a pile of twigs.

"I know you," the pooka said in a perfect imitation of Gwen. "You'll want a nice cup of tea."

Devin stopped and stared at him. "How long have you been following us?"

The pooka merely grinned and fed more branches to the fire.

Devin sighed, reaching for his pack. He'd brought the "Unicorn's Best" along. In fact, a cup of tea would make him feel much better right now. He opened the strings that tied his pack. Bright green eyes blinked up at him. It was the faery, in her small brown animal shape.

The animal crept out of the pack and nudged his hand with its cold little nose. Then the air shimmered, and Weasel was a faery girl once more.

"You," said the pooka, watching her.

"Me," the weasel faery agreed.

The pooka turned to Devin, demanding, "Why has Weasel come along? This was supposed to be *my* adventure."

He sounded so cross and so much like Gwen that Devin began to laugh.

The pooka looked at him, confused. Then he began to laugh as well. "You played a good trick on me, yes? Very funny! Very good!" He was suddenly in excellent humor and whistled as he fed the fire.

When he'd had his tea and a proper meal, Devin felt prepared to carry on. Night had fallen, but it was always nighttime in the Dark Queen's realm. He was terrified to reach the hill, yet desperately impatient, too. Gwen was there. That made it better than all the Seelie Court's marvels. He'd rather be where she was, because right now, half of him was missing.

How strange. Just a few days ago, he would have said they had nothing at all in common. But they were twins—and that, he now realized, was a very strong bond indeed. If Gwen was held under the hill, what life could there be for him above it? He'd get her out if he had to trade himself to the Raven Queen.

He covered the ashes of their fire and shouldered the pack and the harp once more. The pooka jumped up eagerly. "Are you ready now, Devinthornworth?"

"I'm ready," said Devin grimly. Then he turned and took little Weasel's hand. It was delicate and human-shaped, lightly pelted. "You must go back. You mustn't be caught here, in the Dark Queen's realm."

She pulled his hand up to her cheek and rubbed it against her soft brown fur. "Yes, you're right, I'll follow you," she said confusingly.

"No, no, no! Go back to the Seelie Court. I'll come back if I can."

"Yes, all right." She picked up Devin's food sack, prepared to come with him.

Faeries. He would never understand them. What was the point in arguing? Gwen never listened to him, either, nor did Vivien or Elaine. So why should Weasel? Faeries, girls, artists—all so blasted stubborn.

The three travelers continued on, moving slowly through the dark, Pooka striding ahead and Weasel clinging to Devin's side. They passed through a ring of standing stones, half hidden in bracken and gorse. They crossed a bog, where mud pulled at their feet with a sucking sound. They climbed a little rise, and Pooka stopped them, a finger to his lips. "Wait," he whispered. "Get down in the weeds." Devin and Weasel did as they were told. Presently, a troop of little men crossed through the woods below. Their faces were as wrinkled as walnuts, and they wore red caps over their thick white hair.

"They belong to Nicnevin," Pooka explained when the last of them was gone. "Their caps are red because they dip them in blood. Beware of them, human boy."

Devin shuddered. Weasel took his hand again as they traveled on.

The trees were small and twisted here, bent with age, thick with moss. The wind picked up, moaning through the midnight forest with a human-sounding voice. Pooka had gone too far ahead. Devin couldn't even see him now. "Pooka," he called, "how much farther?"

Only the gusting wind answered.

"Pooka, where are you?"

"Right here, Devinthornworth," came the prompt reply. Devin heard the pooka's laughter then as the creature jumped him from behind. The boy was knocked to the stony ground, the harp ripped from his back, as the pooka bound him head to foot with ropes of ivy and vines. The vines tightened as Devin struggled against them, his face pressed into dirt. "Weasel," he said, sputtering leaves, "get out of here, quick as you can!"

She listened this time. She shifted to her animal shape and fled into the darkness.

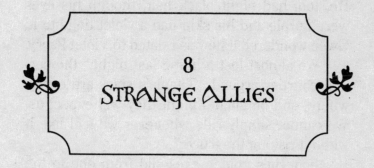

8
STRANGE ALLIES

Gwen's stomach churned the next morning as Violet Faery prodded her into the throne room. She'd actually hoped to be sent straight to the scullery. She couldn't bear to stand there in the Raven Queen's court and watch her kill again.

The ravens were circling low, as if searching for something. They made Gwen nervous. Trying to ignore them, she sought out Thomas. He stood in his place among the courtiers, without the aid of his staff, but there was no color in him at all and she wondered how much longer he could stay upright.

Two of the tall, slender faery courtiers stood before Nicnevin. Gwen remembered seeing them mounted on their chargers in the courtyard, looking as deadly as their queen.

"Tonight is the dark of the moon," the taller

of the two was saying. "Of course, we must ride."
He, too, had night black hair, though his eyes
were purple and his skin had a violet tinge to it.
Gwen wondered if he was related to Violet Faery.

"We almost lost a horse last night," the second courtier argued. "Titania's spies are everywhere, and on such a night they will expect us.
We cannot simply ride whenever we feel like it
without risking the truce."

Nicnevin's golden eyes slid from one to the
other. She inclined her head toward the raven on
her shoulder, which seemed to be having its say,
as well.

"I will not be frightened off by my sister," she
said at last. "Especially on the dark of the moon
when all elements favor the Unseelie Court. We
ride again tonight."

Her sister? Gwen thought. *Are Titania and
Nicnevin sisters?*

Nicnevin gazed across the crowded throne
room, her eyes finding Gwen. "Ah, it's my little
scullery maid. We're so fortunate you came
along. The pots and pans were getting quite out
of hand. Obviously, we needed a mortal captive
to see to them." She darted a golden glance
toward Thomas. "Of course, I thought of him, but
he's really too pretty to waste on such menial
work. Perhaps tonight we shall steal another
mortal to aid you."

"No!" The word was out before Gwen could stop it.

"No?" the Dark Queen queried in a dangerous voice.

Gwen felt her churning stomach knot up, spin some more, and then settle in a giant lump in her throat. Why couldn't she learn not to contradict Nicnevin? Still, she didn't want Nicnevin to steal another mortal—what if the Faery Rade found Devin?

"I—I only meant that I'm sure I can handle the scullery on my own," Gwen said in a voice faint with fear.

Nicnevin laughed, a sound like water running over smooth pebbles. "Yesterday, you only wanted to be an artist, and today you are bound and determined to clean my scullery. What a changeable child you are. Or perhaps it's just a matter of your having found your calling. The Faery Realm can do that, you know—reveal your true nature to you."

This time Gwen resisted telling the Dark Queen that she'd found her calling when she was three and it was *art,* thank you very much.

"Violet Faery, see that she has her wish and return her to the scullery," Nicnevin commanded.

Gwen expected to immediately feel sharp little teeth sink into her, but Violet Faery was again hovering around Thomas. *She must have a special assignment to torment all mortals,* Gwen thought as she started out of the throne room.

Gwen stood up to her armpits in smelly, dirty dishes. It seemed the ones she'd scrubbed the day before were filthy again. Still, she didn't mind half as much as she had the day before. Her mind wasn't on the drudgery but on how she would find food for Thomas.

I must get out from under the hill, she reasoned. Of course, she remembered Thomas's warning that she could no longer survive beyond it. *But I shall stay outside for only a short while,* she told herself. *Just long enough to find something that will keep Thomas alive.*

The problem was, how would she find her way out from under the hill? She somehow doubted that the crystal door would appear for her. Or that Violet Faery would give her leave to go search for it. *Devin would have a plan,* Gwen told herself. *Something very organized and practical...Maybe I could secretly dig my way out of the hill? No, Thomas would probably be dead long before I reached the surface. Perhaps Thomas's mouse would show me a route through the tunnels?* But how to find Thomas? She had no idea where he was kept when he wasn't at Nicnevin's side.

Methodically (for her), Gwen examined and

discarded one plan after another, scouring pots and pans all the while. Above her, the raven circled the scullery, giving her evil looks.

"Why didn't they lose *you* in last night's Rade?" she grumbled. *That's it!* Gwen realized, nearly dropping the pot in her hands. *The Rade! Nicnevin's court will ride out again tonight. I simply have to find a way to slip out with them.*

She then spent the rest of the day trying to devise a plan to do that. By the time the violet faery finally appeared, Gwen had an idea, though she wasn't confident that it would work. How she wished she could ask Devin what he would do.

"Scullery maid!" The faery lit on a stack of clean dishes, her hands on her hips. "You've made no more progress than you did yesterday," she said accusingly.

"Well, it doesn't help to have you leaving tiny violet footprints on the dish I just cleaned," Gwen informed her.

Violet Faery scowled but opened her wings and beat them gently so that she hovered just above the surface of the dish. "Come along," she snapped. "It's time for you to return to your room."

Gwen rinsed off her hands and followed the faery back through the rooms of Nicnevin's palace. *Please let them still be in the courtyard,* she thought. If Nicnevin's knights had already left, she had no hope of getting out.

In the conservatory she saw that the blood red flowers had again been snapped off. And when she and the violet faery entered the courtyard, she saw the blossoms wound through the horses' manes. The riders were gathering in formation with Nicnevin at their head and, behind her, the courtier who'd argued for riding out. He must be one of her captains, Gwen realized.

Gwen knew that she needed to wait until the procession had begun to wind its way out of the hill. She had to be sure that the crystal door would be open.

She took a deep breath and reminded herself that Dev always told her she was the best actress in the family.

"Ow!" she cried loudly. She dropped to the ground with a grimace and began rubbing her ankle.

"Get up!" Violet Faery snapped. "Do you want a horse to trample you?"

"I—I can't," Gwen gasped. She couldn't make her ankle swell, but she shut her eyes and willed herself to cry. She felt the tears at once and glanced up at the faery through welling eyes. "I—I must have twisted it," she sobbed. "I don't think I can put weight on it."

"Do you think I care?" Violet sparks flashed

from the faery's eyes. "Get up now!"

But Gwen had bought the time she needed. The Faery Host had mounted their steeds, and with a jingle of bridles and a clang of spurs, they rode toward the arch in the courtyard wall.

Gwen made a lengthy, tortured production of getting to her feet. *I really am quite a good actress,* she thought.

"Hurry!" Violet Faery snapped, flying on.

Gwen hobbled after her, nearing the arch. The riders' orderly procession was passing under it now, and Gwen could see the crystal door ahead of them. *Time for Act Two,* she decided—and stumbled against one of the porcelain urns, knocking it to the ground.

The urn smashed against the flagstones, making the most awful noise and sending dirt and blue vines flying through the dusky air. Horses reared, terrified, throwing some of the faery knights and forcing the others to fight to stay on. The captain of the Rade wheeled on his mount, barking orders that could scarcely be heard above the din—and Gwen sprinted through the archway. Just ahead of her, she saw the rock crystal door, opening to the night. Instinctively, she leaped, tucked herself into a tight ball, and rolled through the doorway and then down the side of the hill.

It was a long, bumping, thumping way, but at

last she tumbled to a stop at the base of a thorn-bush. Slowly, Gwen uncurled herself and plucked a thorn from her side. She felt bruised all over, but that was the least of her worries. Would the Faery Host come searching for her? Surely, Violet Faery would tell them that she'd deliberately broken the urn and then escaped during the confusion. Gwen found herself shaking as she realized how furious Nicnevin would be when she discovered she'd been tricked.

So she crawled a little deeper into the woods, where she huddled beneath a rowan tree. It reminded her of the tree in her tapestry, and she felt that was a hopeful sign. She stayed very still, taking in the sweet woodsy scents of damp earth, trees, and the flowers that covered the forest floor. Somewhere nearby, she heard the sound of running water.

The ringing sound of bridles soon snapped her to attention. It was so dark beneath the moonless sky and trees that she could barely see, but she heard hoofbeats, spurs and armor jangling, and bell-like laughter—the Faery Rade was abroad.

Please don't let them find me, she prayed. *Please don't let them find me.*

They did not even ride in her direction. The noise faded into the distance, leaving only the sounds of the forest—crickets chirping, the stream running, and somewhere, an owl calling. She was alone.

Which means that I must now find food for Thomas, Gwen resolved. *Which would be a lot easier with a lantern.*

She stretched out a hand and began to feel around the forest floor. She found acorns. Squirrels ate acorns, but could you feed them to a human? Perhaps not. A slimy toadstool? Better not—growing this close to the Unseelie Court, it was probably poison. Green leaves that smelled like wild mint—that was a start, at least. Gwen plucked a handful of the wild mint and decided to walk toward the sound of the stream. Animals always seemed to feed near water; there was a good chance she'd find something edible there.

Again, she found herself wishing Devin were along. Dev was forever picking up bizarre facts— like how to find edible roots in the wild—from all those boring books he read.

Gwen moved between the trees, careful to keep the faery hill in sight. The land was relatively flat, yet she felt as if she were walking uphill. She was winded and exhausted, though she'd barely traveled thirty yards. *It's because I ate their food and left their realm,* she realized with a rising sense of panic. *That's why they didn't bother to send anyone after me. They knew I'd never last out here.*

She forced herself to push on. She simply refused to have come this far only to let Thomas die. She pulled up some dandelions and stuffed them into the waistband of her apron. Nanny Swan was always trying to get the flock of Swans to eat boiled dandelion greens. They must be good for something.

Gwen was panting by the time she reached the stream. So before looking for more food, she kneeled, cupped some water in her hand, and drank it down. The water was clear and icy and tasted of honey and flowers. Gwen felt the exhaustion leave her body and her breathing slow. The water was giving her new strength.

"I must bring some back for Thomas," she said aloud. But of course, she hadn't thought to bring a pitcher or even a cup. What could she use to carry the water? She glanced around. "Maybe I could weave some rushes into a basket," she murmured.

"Rushes don't grow on these banks, and yet *you're* going to weave a watertight basket of them? In the dark? Tell me, mortal, could you have come up with a more useless idea?"

Gwen's heart sank as a tiny violet light glowed in front of her. "You stupid, clumsy girl!" the faery shrieked. "You caused all that chaos in the Lady's courtyard. And for what—so you could learn basket weaving?"

"Leave me alone," Gwen said, choking back tears.

"You're lucky I found you, because you won't survive outside the hill another hour. Even that stream water can't keep you alive. *And who's Thomas?*"

Gwen fell silent with surprise. He'd never told the Unseelie Court his name.

Violet Faery tugged at the dandelion leaves caught between Gwen's apron and skirt. "The other mortal!" she said softly. "You're bringing him food!"

"He'll die without it," Gwen said bleakly.

"Then you'd better find him something more palatable," the faery snapped.

"What?" Gwen couldn't believe she'd heard that correctly.

But Violet Faery was busily digging at the ground. She moved with blinding speed, and in a few moments had unearthed several pearl white roots. Then she flitted across the forest floor and returned with a cache of nuts and berries.

"Hold out your apron, girl," she ordered Gwen.

Too astounded to argue, Gwen obeyed, and the faery began to fill her apron with nuts and berries and roots, wild mint, and even a large glistening honeycomb.

"You were actually right about one thing," the

faery said resentfully, her wings beating in an
angry blur. "He needs water." Without warning,
she grabbed the hem of Gwen's skirt, sank her
sharp little teeth into it, and ripped off a good-
sized swatch of cloth. Gwen watched in mute
astonishment as the faery smeared the cloth with
silt from the bottom of the stream, fashioned it
into the shape of large mug, then ordered it to
dry, "swift and right and watertight." A bright
violet glow surrounded the mug. When the glow
faded, the faery said, "Fill it with water, you lazy
girl. And then it's back to the hill, and no
dawdling!"

Gwen finally found her voice. "Why are you
doing this?"

"Because *you* clearly weren't capable." The
faery pinched Gwen's arm. "Hurry now. He
doesn't have much time left!"

Careful to keep the precious food from falling
out of her apron, Gwen kneeled by the steam and
filled the mug with sweet cold water.

The violet faery flew ahead, forcing Gwen to
hurry to keep up with her. When at last they
reached the hill, the faery beat her wings
together in song, and the crystal door opened.

"This way," Violet Faery said, flying into one
of the mole tunnels.

Gwen felt a sickening sense of fear fill her as
she re-entered the hill—though she also felt the

weakness lift. "Wait," she called out. "I have to know. Did you tell Nicnevin I escaped?"

"I didn't even tell her you knocked over the urn," Violet Faery answered.

"And how do I know I can believe you?" Gwen asked, her voice shaking.

"Because we are not like your kind." The faery's voice was cold with contempt. "Whatever else we may do, good or ill, we never speak an untruth. To do so goes against the very power that is our magic. Besides," she added a bit more sullenly, "Nicnevin would not be pleased with me if she knew a prisoner in my charge had caused such chaos."

"And why are you helping Thomas?"

The faery didn't answer, but her violet color deepened to a dark purple.

She's blushing! Gwen realized, astounded. "You fancy him, don't you!" she said.

"Don't you?" the faery retorted.

"Well, yes," Gwen admitted, "but not seriously. I'm only twelve. He's far too old for me."

"And too large for me," the faery said with a sigh. "Still, he's the handsomest being ever to enter the hill, and there's something—kind—about him."

"Imagine that!" Gwen muttered. "You actually know what kindness is."

That earned Gwen another sharp pinch from

the faery (apparently her regard for kindness applied only to Thomas), who then flew on. Gwen followed her through endless branches of the winding tunnels. It was a wonder, she thought, that the faeries themselves didn't get lost in this place.

At last, Violet Faery stopped before an arched wooden door and pushed it open. Gwen stepped inside and saw the Rhymer slumped against a wall in an odd position—as if he'd fallen. She hurried to his side. "Thomas! Thomas, are you all right?"

He didn't answer. His eyes were closed, his face drawn and white.

"Of course he's not all right!" Violet Faery snapped. "Do stop wasting time and feed him!"

Gwen glared at the faery but said gently to Thomas, "We brought you water and food. From outside the hill. Please, you must try to eat some of it." She held the mug of water to his mouth and let a few drops of the precious liquid fall on his lips, then a few more.

Thomas stirred and raised his head. "My lady?" he asked, sounding confused. Gwen wondered who he meant, though Violet Faery landed on his collarbone, as though she were sure he meant her. "Drink the water," she urged him. *"Please."*

Very slowly, Thomas drank the water, then ate some honey. He smiled when Violet Faery handed him a blackberry, and ate that, too. "Thank you," he said at last.

Gwen helped him to his feet so he could sit in the room's large chair, whose carved arms and legs were in the shape of intertwined serpents. Thomas's room had finer furnishings than hers, she noted. The bed was draped with silk curtains, the table was larger—its trestles were carved bear cubs standing on their hind legs—and he actually had a looking glass while her room had none.

The violet faery flitted around Thomas and tenderly brushed a strand of hair from his forehead. "You must keep eating to regain your strength."

The Rhymer regarded her with curiosity. "I wouldn't have thought you'd go foraging for food to feed a captive mortal."

"I also made the cup," Violet Faery informed him proudly. She gave Gwen a contemptuous toss of her head. "*She* wanted to weave rushes."

Thomas ignored that. "Weren't you afraid of angering your queen?"

Gwen spoke up. "Leaving the hill to find you food was my idea, actually." She could take only so much of the nasty little creature's acting as though she were the sole reason Thomas was alive. "Violet Faery only came after me because she thought I ran away."

"Don't be absurd," the faery said. "Why would I chase after you? I knew you'd have to return to the hill."

"But you didn't want Nicnevin to know you'd lost your charge," Gwen pointed out.

"And *you* couldn't find a blackberry in the forest if it popped into your mouth!" the faery countered.

Thomas gave a low chuckle, and Violet Faery turned her flashing eyes on him. "And what, may I ask, is so humorous?"

He bit back a grin. "I hope neither one of you will take offense at this, but in certain ways...you're very much alike."

"Eeew!" Gwen turned her back on him in disgust, and Violet Faery made a retching sound.

"I meant it as a compliment," the Rhymer added quickly. "You're both very strong-willed, very beautiful, and very brave. I'm honored by your friendship." He helped himself to a walnut and winked at Gwen. "Real food—what a wonderful, *practical* idea!"

The violet faery scowled at the girl. "It's time you returned to your room, mortal," she announced.

"Go with her," Thomas said to Gwen when he

saw that she was about to object.

Gwen nodded. "I'm glad you're feeling better," she told the Rhymer. "Good night."

The violet faery was silent as she led Gwen through the warren of tunnels, and Gwen was grateful. She had no desire for another exchange of insults with the faery. She was suddenly, overwhelmingly weary. In fact, she was so tired that at first she thought her eyes were playing tricks on her when she saw it—a green-eyed mink—scrambling along one of the branches of the tunnel. She looked again, and the mink skittered frantically in the opposite direction. *Poor little thing*, Gwen thought. *It burrowed into the hill by mistake, and now it's as lost as the rest of us.*

"Are you coming?" Violet Faery demanded impatiently.

"Yes," Gwen replied, and she actually did hurry. She couldn't wait to close her eyes in that hard, lumpy bed.

Gwen entered the throne room the next morning with trepidation. Perhaps Violet Faery hadn't told Nicnevin about her escape, but that didn't mean the Dark Queen didn't know. Her ravens were everywhere, and Gwen had spent a restless night, convinced that one of them had seen her escape. It didn't help that they were now circling the throne room, as if searching for carrion.

She forgot her own fears, though, when she saw that the usual courtiers were not standing alongside the throne. The Rhymer was not in his usual place.

Thomas! Gwen felt her heart constrict. *Had something happened to Thomas? Or had they simply been too late in getting him food?*

It was impossible to tell by looking at the Raven Queen. Nicnevin sat on her throne, calmly consulting with a circle of tiny faeries who hovered in front of her.

A sudden flurry rippled through the court as a small furry creature skittered across the tile floor and beneath Nicnevin's throne.

"Catch it!" shouted a tall faery who looked like nothing so much as a giant upright frog, complete with green skin and webbed hands and feet.

Gwen craned her head and saw that the frog faery was chasing the little mink she'd seen the night before. *Oh, why did you have to run into the throne room?* she asked it silently.

The mink darted out from under the throne, round the base of one of the golden columns, then under the long pink skirt of a faery girl, who gave a loud shriek that finally caused Nicnevin to look up from her conference.

"Enough," the Dark Queen said.

She raised a hand, and two of her ravens flew

down from the columns. Within seconds, they caught the little mink.

They held it aloft in their sharp beaks, waiting for their queen's command.

Gwen thought she was going to be violently ill. She couldn't bear to watch them tear apart another helpless creature.

But Nicnevin said in a calm, melodious voice, "I have need of a footstool, little weasel. You'll do quite nicely."

The ravens dropped the struggling creature. It fell to the tiled floor, landing as a small wooden footstool, perfectly carved in the shape of a mink.

Gwen blinked, trying hard to believe what she'd just seen. Something Thomas said came back to her: "Every mortal creature here is her prisoner." And then she understood—all of the animals in the fabulously carved furniture that filled the palace…they were not carvings at all.

"That's better," Nicnevin said as the two lines of courtiers entered the throne room. Gwen nearly went weak with relief when she saw Thomas among them. He was still much too thin, but looked ever so much better than he had the day before. He no longer struggled to hold himself upright, and there was some color in his face.

The Raven Queen noticed it, too. "Come here, mortal," she said.

Thomas stepped forward with that unshakable calm of his. Gwen couldn't imagine how it was that he managed to show no fear. "You look much improved," Nicnevin told him. "Perhaps I might ascribe this change to a restful night's sleep?"

"On that wondrously comfortable bed," Thomas agreed, his voice heavy with sarcasm.

"I'm so glad you're enjoying your stay," Nicnevin replied cordially. Then she looked past him, and her eyes sought out Gwenevere. "Come here, girl," she commanded.

Gwen froze. She knew she should obey, but every muscle in her body was locked with terror.

"I said, *come here!*" The Dark Queen's voice thundered through the throne room.

Gwen shot a panicked look at Thomas and was surprised when he gazed back at her with a calm, steady look that actually gave her courage. It was as if in that glance he held out a hand to her and said, "You're not alone in this. You have a friend."

Just put one foot in front of the other, Gwen told herself. Slowly, she crossed the throne room and took her place in front of the Raven Queen.

Nicnevin's eyes danced with golden fire. "How dare you give sustenance to one who should eat only from my table? Did you think I wouldn't notice?"

Gwen couldn't find words to answer. The

ravens had dropped lower. Now they circled only inches above her head.

Nicnevin rose to her feet and spread her own black wings. They stretched nearly to the sides of the room and seemed to engulf the great hall in darkness. Gwen felt her knees knocking together in pure terror.

"I have been much too lenient with you," Nicnevin went on in a velvety voice, "but I shall remedy that now. Stretch out your arms, mortal."

Gwen's arms shook as she stretched them out. Was this so the ravens could tear her apart more easily?

"At last you obey," the Dark Queen said with a smile. Then she pointed at Gwen and spoke an ancient word of power.

Gwen felt her lips harden and lengthen, her back contract and curve. A sharp pain streaked through each foot, and her toes became thin, spindly claws. Her legs seemed to collapse in on themselves until her body was only a short distance from the floor. And her arms—shiny black feathers were sprouting from each arm.

"Stop!" Gwen cried in horror. But her shout came out as a harsh caw. Her only protest was an indignant flap of her wings.

Gwen was now one of the Dark Queen's ravens.

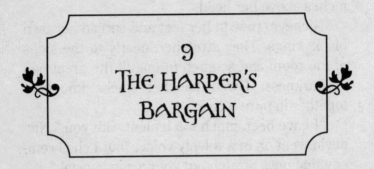

9
THE HARPER'S BARGAIN

The pooka flung Devin over one shoulder and carried him off like a sack of potatoes, leaving the splintered harp behind. The boy was still bound head and foot, bruised and furious. He gritted his teeth as he was conveyed in this awkward, undignified fashion. He'd known all along that the pooka was not to be trusted. Oberon would banish the creature, but would that even matter to him? The pooka would laugh and return to the hall of his true mistress, Nicnevin.

The night was pitch-black, but this did not slow the pooka's progress through the forest. Weasel was nowhere to be seen, and for this, at least, Devin was grateful. The faery girl had escaped. Perhaps she was already on her way to the Seelie Court to warn Titania and Oberon of what had happened. But what did that matter?

They'd already told him they would not risk war for mortal captives. Oberon would have to send word to the Aislings to warn them away from the island. No doubt, he'd also send word to the *Basset* that the Thornworth twins were lost to the world and would never return from under the hill. The *Basset* would sail away without them, giving them up for dead.

Pooka stopped abruptly, dropping the boy in a pile of leaves and dirt. The air shimmered, and a huge black dog with red eyes stood over Devin. A grassy hill loomed above like the ancient burial mounds of Cornwall. Ravens circled in the night sky, black shadows against the stars.

The dog barked loudly—once, twice, three times. A door in the hillside opened. The door was elaborately carved from rock crystal but marred with lichen and moss. A faery stood in the entranceway, the ugliest one that Devin had seen, with a long furry snout, misshapen feet, and a rat's tail that dragged on the floor. The pooka changed to goat-man shape, his horsey teeth stretched in a wide grin. He swaggered. "Got a present here, I do, for the Raven Queen."

The guardsman scratched his snout and said, "Wha' issit?"

"I'll tell that to the Queen and only the Queen. Now, out of my way!" The pooka picked Devin up again, pushed the clumsy guard aside, and entered the hill, hooves striking against bare stone down a damp passageway.

Devin saw faces, each stranger than the next, staring and whispering. Hands pinched and pulled him as he passed, and he heard peals of laughter, including the pooka's. His heart clenched, thinking of Gwenevere in this terrible place.

The pooka carried him up and up an endless series of winding stairs. At the very top was a vast chamber. Ravens circled overhead. All conversation stopped as the pooka laid Devin at the feet of his Queen.

She sat upon a golden throne with wild-eyed deer carved into the arms. Her face was Titania's face—but there all similarity between them ended. Nicnevin's hair was black as coal, her skin white as milk, her lips red as blood. She was heartbreakingly beautiful, a thing the boy had not expected. But her golden eyes, cool and amused, held cruelty in their depths.

"What have you brought me today, Pooka?" she said in a rich, melodious voice.

"Quite a prize," the pooka boasted, strutting before the Queen's dais.

She lifted a slender hand in dismissal. "Another mortal. I already have some. They're more trouble than they're worth, I've decided."

"Ah, but this one is worth his weight in gold,

silver, and rubies, too. You'll want this one. His name is Thomas the Rhymer, and he is a harper."

The Raven Queen sat forward, her eyes glittering with interest now. "Indeed. Pooka, you amaze me. Where did you find this interesting creature?"

"I stole him away from the Seelie Court." He gave her a grin with many large teeth.

She laughed, delighted. "Oh, you've done well. Untie the mortal and let me see him!"

Two filthy faeries crept forward and chewed through Devin's bindings with their sharp little teeth. Devin winced as he sat up, every bump and bruise and scratch protesting. He felt two hands grab him under the arms, and the pooka set him on his feet. Devin caught his eye, and the pooka winked. Whose side was this creature on?

"Bow to the Queen," Pooka said grandly.

Devin complied as best he could. The Queen was watching him eagerly, a hunger in her eyes. Her courtiers, arrayed behind her, were watching him intently as well. One in particular had his gaze riveted on Devin's face.

"Your fame precedes you," the Raven Queen said. "Let's see if your skill is equal to it...Bring this mortal a harp!" she called. A magnificent harp of willow wood was quickly produced. "Now give us a song, Rhymer. You see, my entire court awaits you."

Devin made the mistake of looking around at the hundreds of faeries gathered there—big and small, handsome and hideous, eager and scornful. The boy's hands were shaking. He took a deep breath. *This is for Gwen,* he told himself firmly. He had a role to play, and the pooka seemed to be helping him.

"Your Majesty," Devin said in a confident voice that was quite unlike his own, "I am indeed a harper and, yes, I have a certain skill. But is this the way you treat harpers in your hall? Like a slave or a servant boy? What of the Harper's Law, Lady?"

She shrugged. "What do I care for laws?"

"So you'd rather have all harpers tell the tale of the Raven Queen's sad little court, poor and paltry, unable to pay the proper Harper's Fee? Very well. Then I'll begin," he said slyly.

"Wait, mortal," said Nicnevin. "What is this Harper's Fee you speak of?"

"Only this: If I please you, Lady, you'll pay whatever I ask of you."

"Whatever?" Nicnevin frowned at this. She glanced at Pooka, who nodded.

"That's the Harper's Fee and the Harper's Law," Devin lied smoothly, casually examining the harp in his hands. "But if you can't afford it, of course…"

"I'll pay your Harper's Fee," the Queen

snarled, "should your songs prove to be worth anything. But I warn you, mortal, you must please me first. And I am not easily pleased. Should you fail to amuse and amaze my court, then I swear I'll give you to my ravens—and they can feast on those nimble fingers you think so highly of."

"Done!" said Devin, and he spoke a magical word in the old language of the faeries—one that would seal this bargain between them. Nicnevin's eyes narrowed dangerously. Oberon had taught him that word.

"Play, mortal!" she said angrily. "Play! My ravens are waiting for you."

He sat down on a wooden footstool shaped like a little brown animal. He looked around the court once more, searching the crowd for Gwenevere. There was no sign of his sister, and even the pooka had now disappeared.

"I grow impatient," said the Queen.

"Then I will begin," he said gallantly. When he placed his hands on the willow wood harp, they seemed to take on a life of their own, and a ripple of music filled the hall, as sweet as any ever heard. Devin paused. The hall was utterly still as the delicate notes died slowly away. And then he began to play in earnest, his fingers dancing over the strings.

He knew (from his reading on board the *Bas-*

set) that faeries relished three kinds of music: *gentrai,* which were the songs of joy; *goltrai,* the songs of sorrow; and *suantri,* the songs of healing and magic. He played all three, moving the faeries from laughter to grief to pure enchantment. Then, plucking a quieter tune, the boy began to sing.

He sang of the Scotsman called Glenkindie, who could harp the fish out of the water, and of the Finnish hero Gunnar, whose harping held death at bay. He sang of the Russian czar held prisoner by a wicked Saracen, and the brave czarina who won him back again with her musical skill. He sang of the poor girl drowned by a jealous rival whose body floated to land—where her breastbone was made into a harp, strung with her yellow hair. When the harp was played at her rival's wedding, it spoke aloud with the drowned girl's voice, telling all the wedding guests about the bride's treachery.

He finished with The Maid on the Shore, who was lured onto a sailing ship by a wicked captain, who meant to sail away with the pretty girl. The girl played sweetly on her harp, and soon all the sailors were fast asleep. Then she robbed them of their gold and rowed back to the shore.

Nicnevin roared with laughter at the exploits of the clever maid—and Devin nearly swooned with relief. The music was winning her over! He finished with a merry jig that had the faeries on their feet, stamping time and twirling each other about in a wild frenzy. But when the music ended, the room fell quiet. No faery dared to applaud. Every head turned toward the Raven Queen to follow her lead.

The Queen sat stroking one of her birds, which trembled under her white hand. "Very good," said the Queen at last.

Devin let out the breath he'd been holding. "Then I shall name my fee and go."

"Not so fast. I am not yet fully pleased," said the Raven Queen. She looked like a cat with a nice fat mouse. "You are known for your stories as well as your songs. Now tell a story to me."

A story? No one had said a thing about telling stories to the Queen. Oberon's spell gave him skill with the harp, it gave him magical ballads to sing…but it didn't make him a storyteller. He swallowed nervously. "There are stories in my songs, Lady. Perhaps another—"

"No," she said. "You sing the old ballads well, Rhymer. But I want something different now. A story. Weave me a story. Come, amuse me if you can."

"Um, very well," Devin improvised. What on earth was he going to do? He told them to take the harp away, just to buy a little more time. He loved stories—he'd read hundreds of them—but now he couldn't remember a single one! The court was waiting. *Don't think about all those watching eyes,* he told himself. *Just think about Gwen. Just think what she would do and say.*

He opened his mouth, hoping somehow that Oberon's magic spell would work. Nothing came out. The Queen looked bored, then cross, and the faeries tittered.

His mind raced. What could he say? The Queen began to rise to her feet. *Say anything,* he told himself, *just get her back in that chair!*

"A storm was coming," he shouted out. Then, in a more reasonable tone, he went on, "but the winds were still, and in the wild woods of Broceliande, before an oak tree so hollow huge and old it looked like a tower of ivied masonwork, at Merlin's feet the wily Vivien lay—"

"Very nice," Nicnevin interrupted dryly, "but I've read Mr. Tennyson's poems. You must please me with a *new* story. Give me one or lose our bargain, Rhymer."

Devin wiped the sweat from his brow. His eyes strayed toward the courtiers. The skinny one, staring at him, was mouthing a word. *Gwenevere.*

Devin's eyes snapped back to the Queen. "I'll tell you the story of Gwenevere."

"Yes, yes, I know about Queen Guinevere," the Dark Queen said crossly.

"Not King Arthur's Guinevere," Devin said with a true harper's arrogance, "but a mortal maid on a magical quest with...with...with a raven on her shoulder," he blurted. Nicnevin looked interested now. "And a tall white horse... and a small brown mink..." He was thinking of Gwenevere's tapestry. "No, not a mink. A weasel! But a very wonderful weasel, with eyes of green. Once upon a time, in a land far away, where all magic was fast asleep, a girl named Gwenevere lay in her bed with a terrible fever..."

From that hesitant opening, the story took on a life all its own. The tale was like those little faery lights, fluttering just up ahead, and Devin was merely following it—through the door of his sister's tapestry into a world of magic and myth, where it became an adventure that held its listeners utterly spellbound.

He forgot all the eyes watching him, he forgot himself, he forgot about Gwen, he just followed the tale...full of manticores and faeries and dwarves and other familiar things...but also full of surprises...laughter...danger...sorrow...and delight. He heard gasps when dragons filled the skies, sobs when a wise old unicorn died, and cheers when the bold young Gwenevere found her way back home at last. When he came to the very end of the tale, he blinked and recalled where he was. Not in the land of the tapestry, not safe at home in St. Ives, either, but in the Dark Queen's hall, with ravens circling overhead.

This time, the court did not wait for their queen. They cheered and hollered and stamped and whistled. The Raven Queen was silent, furtively brushing a tear from her eye.

Devin kneeled before the throne. "Has my story pleased you, Your Majesty?"

She looked as if she would prefer to deny it— but a Faery Queen's word is a Faery Queen's law. "You did," she said at last. "Truly, your fame is earned, Thomas the Rhymer."

He raised his head, looked her in the eye. "Then let me claim my Harper's Fee."

"Rise, mortal, and tell me what it shall be. I have gold and silver in store, jewels and rubies beyond compare. Or take the harp you played, made by Taliesin, the greatest of all the bards. Not since he walked these lands have I heard a story so fine as yours."

Devin rose and stood squarely before Nic- nevin. "These things are much too grand for me. I want only the mortal girl who's captive in your hall."

The Faery Queen's eyes flashed dangerously. "How do you know of this mortal girl?"

"The tales of your exploits are renowned far and wide," Devin said cunningly. "And as a teller of tales, I make it my business to listen to them."

"I see," said Nicnevin tightly. She was not pleased by the harper's request. "What do you want with that useless runt of a mortal? She's not worth anything."

Devin shrugged casually, as though the prize were little indeed. "I fancy a servant to cook and clean for me, and she'll do nicely, that's all."

"I'll give you a faery," said Nicnevin. "I'll give you a dozen to choose among."

"A faery?" said Devin, pretending shock. "Oh, no, Lady, it wouldn't do. A faery to serve a mere mortal?"

"Yes, yes, you have a point." Nicnevin rose from her golden chair and paced the dais it sat upon. "Choose something else, harper. I have great wonders in my treasure room. Seven-league boots. Cloaks of invisibility. Wallets that never empty. Choose one of these, and you shall be a friend of the Unseelie Court."

"I've made my choice," said Devin calmly. "And I want the mortal girl—just as she was when she entered this hill, along with safe passage for us both. I want no quarrels following me when I leave your gracious hall."

"Do you think your story worth so much?" the Queen snapped.

"It seems to me, Lady, that I ask for very little from you. What is one useless mortal compared to the treasures of Nicnevin's realm?"

Nicnevin scowled, her eyes flashing. And then the Dark Queen smiled at Devin. He didn't like that smile or the sudden sweetness in her tone. "All right, then, take the girl and go. She's in this hall right now, Rhymer. Take her if you can..."

"And if I do," Devin bargained, "will we be safe from you and your court?"

"Find her," the Queen bargained in turn, "and I shall grant safe passage to you, Thomas, and the mortal girl." Her smile was treacherous, as though she'd won the bargain already.

Devin's eyes whipped round the crowded room. There was, of course, no sign of Gwen. Had she been turned into a faery—one of these strange, misshapen things? And if she had, how would he ever know which one she was? He looked toward the skinny courtier who had silently mouthed his sister's name, but the man was pale, his eyes squeezed tightly shut as if with pain.

Devin looked round the room again, and a hundred faeries looked back at him. "Choose me!" "Choose me!" "Choose me!" they shouted, jostling each other and laughing raucously. A big black dog slipped through the crowd and stared at him with flame red eyes. Then it barked— once, twice, three times—setting the ravens squawking above.

The Raven Queen was enjoying herself. She watched Devin with gleaming eyes. Her hideous birds were swooping over her throne, flapping their wings at the barking dog. Except for one. It sat on the Queen's shoulder, its head cocked to one side. It stared at Devin out of one bold eye. And then he knew.

"There's the mortal girl," he said, pointing to the raven on the Queen's shoulder.

The smile left Nicnevin's face, and she leapt to her feet. "You wretch! You poxy, short-lived thing! Who told you? How did you know?

"I'd recognize my sister anywhere," said Devin.

"Your sister!"

He stood and faced her wrath. "Now you owe us safe passage, Lady. Does the Raven Queen honor her word?"

"Take the wretched bird with you and leave my court at once, Mortal!"

"The girl must be as she was when she entered this hill," Devin reminded her.

Nicnevin screamed aloud with rage. But she was bound by the bargain she'd made, by magic as old as the Realm. She pointed at the bird and said a single word of power in the old language, and the bird became a girl in a muddy, jeweled dress, feathers in her hair.

She was a beautiful sight. Devin grabbed his

sister's chapped red hands in his. "Come, let's go," he said urgently.

"Wait, we have to bring Thomas, too. He's weak. He's going to need our help..." Gwen broke away from his grasp.

Thomas? Devin watched as she ran to the side of the skinny courtier.

"Leave him be!" the Queen ordered.

Gwen turned, her own eyes flashing. "Remember your words, Lady. You said: 'I grant safe passage to you, Thomas, and the mortal girl.' That's *three* of us. The harper is my brother, Devin. *This* is Thomas the Rhymer, and we're taking him with us."

"What!" Nicnevin blazed with fury, her eyes moving from Thomas to Devin...and then to Pooka, for he had brought the false harper into her hall. Pooka gazed right back at her, a smile on his canine face.

"You!" sputtered the Raven Queen.

"Me," the big black dog agreed. "It was a good trick, wasn't it?"

"Come with us, Pooka," Devin pleaded, moving between the pooka and the Queen. "We need your help again, for Thomas. You're stronger than any of us."

The dog turned flaming eyes on the boy; then he seemed to melt into thin air. In his place, a huge white horse pranced on the tiles. Together,

Devin and Gwen helped the harper onto its back. "Hold on," Gwen told the man. He nodded weakly and leaned on the horse's neck as it clattered away.

She turned to her brother. "All right, Dev, let's get out of this blasted hill."

The faeries couldn't hurt them now, but they pushed and jeered and shouted and shrieked, and the ravens dove over their heads while their mistress watched and glowered darkly, her eyes narrowed with hatred.

Gwen suddenly turned, ran back to the Dark Queen's throne, and grabbed the footstool sitting there.

"Leave it. Are you daft?" said Devin. "Come on! We don't need a souvenir!"

But she held on to it stubbornly as they made their way down the endless stairs, a troop of faeries at their heels all the way to the crystal door.

The horse stood in the opening, preventing the door from swinging shut. He held it while the children passed, and he followed after them. The door closed with a muffled thud. And then there was no sign of it.

Just a hill, grass wet with dew. Titania's doves were circling. The sun was rising through the trees, turning night into day.

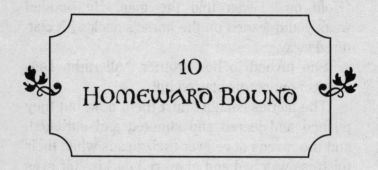

10
HOMEWARD BOUND

Gwen ran toward the rising sun, Devin by her side, and the white horse carrying Thomas, ahead of them. The mink footstool was tucked beneath one of her arms. It was cumbersome running along the winding forest paths, wearing a jeweled dress and carrying a wooden footstool, but she didn't care. Titania's doves flew overhead, and the air was fresh and sweet. All that mattered was getting as far from the Unseelie Court as possible. They were free of the Raven Queen. Wondrously, gloriously free!

The path wound downhill, and Gwen found herself short of breath. She slowed down.

Devin noticed at once. "What's wrong?" he asked, slowing his pace to match hers.

"I don't know," Gwen answered—and then she realized that she *did* know.

"Gwen?" Dev looked worried.

Gwen swallowed hard. "I—I don't understand why it's happening," she said in a shaky voice. "Nicnevin promised I would be as I was when I entered the hill, and it was only after that I—it's not fair that this is happening again!"

"What's not fair? What's happening again?" Devin glanced up as the white horse trotted back to them.

Gwen's words came out in a broken whisper. "When I was under the hill, I ate their food. Now I—I can't last outside their realm."

"Oh, Gwen." Devin's eyes reflected her own grief. "Then…all that was for nothing. What are we going to do? Do you want us to take you back?"

The girl shuddered. "No! I'd rather die here with you than be anywhere near the Unseelie Court."

"Mortals and their talk of death!" the pooka snorted. "You're all so fascinated by it! Devinthornworth, this is not a matter for discussion. Take her to Titania!"

"I can't—" Gwen started to protest, but fainted before she could finish the thought.

Gwen woke to the sound of lilting harp music and the feel of something cold and metallic. She opened her eyes and shrieked. Nicnevin sat by her side, rolling a small but heavy golden ball across her forehead.

"Don't!" Gwen yelped, and tried to sit up.

"Rest easy, Gwenevere." The Faery Queen pushed her gently back onto a bed made of the softest green moss.

No, it wasn't Nicnevin, Gwen realized. The woman at her side had Nicnevin's elegant bone structure but hair that shimmered pearl white, like the inside of a shell. And there was kindness in her eyes instead of cruelty.

"I am Titania," the faery woman said in answer to the girl's unasked question. "And I am so very glad to meet you at last." She continued to calmly roll the golden sphere across Gwen's body, murmuring words in an ancient tongue.

"Another song, my lady?"

Gwen turned her head toward the familiar voice. "Thomas!" The Rhymer sat comfortably on a moss-covered tree stump, playing his harp. Thomas winked at her, but his smile was for Titania, and Gwen suddenly understood. "When Violet Faery and I found you nearly unconscious, it was Titania you meant when you said 'my lady,' wasn't it?"

Thomas nodded and plucked a lighter tune. "My songs have always been for her. That's why I could never play for Nicnevin. Every note would have been a betrayal."

Titania rolled the golden ball down each of Gwen's legs and over her feet. "There." She held the golden sphere in her palm for a moment and whispered to it. The metal ball rose like a soap bubble and floated up through a ring of white doves and into the trees.

Gwen watched the golden sphere disappear into the skies. It seemed so familiar to her, like something from her dreams. "What was that golden ball?" she couldn't help asking.

"The golden sphere is used in healing," the Faery Queen answered. "In this case, it removed the curse of the hill from you. You will no longer weaken from having eaten the fruits of my sister's realm."

Gwen blinked. "I don't understand why the curse stayed with me. Nicnevin promised to return me to as I was when I entered her realm."

"Not everything that happens in Nicnevin's realm is her doing," Titania explained. "Nicnevin could only reverse her own spells. But you ate food taken from the hill, and it was the hill itself that then held power over you. None of us exist apart from the land we dwell on, child. Faeries especially are so closely linked that sometimes we are but a reflection of it."

"Then the golden sphere—?"

"For longer than any can remember, the earth of the hill has been filled with darkness and devastation," Titania went on. "The only thing that can counter it is something taken from the earth of the Seelie Court."

"I think it once cured me of a high fever," Gwen murmured, more to herself than to Titania. She knew why it seemed familiar. It was the golden sphere from the tapestry. She envisioned the scene beneath the rowan tree—the white horse, the raven, the mink, the golden ball in the girl's hand—and it seemed to her that the tapestry had always held the secrets of her journey to both faery courts. And, of course, Devin must have known that, for those were the elements he wove together in the story he told for the Unseelie Court.

"Please, my lady," Gwen said. "Do you know where my brother is?"

Titania inclined her head toward a grove of ancient oak trees. "He is speaking with my lord, Oberon."

Gwen got to her feet and gazed around. She was still in the forest, but in the ruins of a crumbling palace. Wild roses and honeysuckle twined round broken columns. Moss and ivy covered stone archways, tumbledown walls, and fragments of stairs. All of it seemed ancient, belonging to a much older world. The dress she now wore also seemed to have come from that ancient place—a simple white silk gown that flowed when she moved, light and radiant as a summer morning. It reminded Gwen of Miranda's dress.

She turned to Titania. "And the portrait of the Aisling sisters?"

"Already on the way to their father. Professor Aisling will be delighted to see his daughters looking so well. Thank you for keeping it safe, child."

Gwen felt herself coloring with shame. "Actually, I didn't. It was luck, and the gremlins' foresight, and Devin's making such a brilliant bargain that kept it safe."

"You should tell your brother that," Titania said. "It would be good for Devin to hear such praise from you."

"Yes, I will. At once," Gwen resolved. But as she started toward the oak grove, she saw the little mink footstool. It was leaning against a broken stone step, as though someone had carelessly dropped it there.

Gwen kneeled down, righted it, and stroked its smooth, polished surface. "Don't worry," she told it. "I will ask Titania if she can change you back. After all, she removed the hill's curse from me."

She heard Devin's voice coming from the oak grove. He sounded upset. "Lord Oberon, I haven't seen her since Pooka, here, tied me up."

Gwen neared the trees and saw the pooka,

who was now a man from the waist up, grinning. "What's the problem?" he asked Devin in an innocent tone. "You told her to leave, so she did. You should be pleased that she listened to you at all."

Who are they talking about? Gwen wondered.

"I told her to come back to the Seelie Court," Devin said a bit defensively. "And she said, all right. But she also said, all right, she'd follow me. It was...confusing."

Oberon smiled. "Faeries frequently are. It's our nature, boy."

Dev looked positively distressed. "Are you *sure* she hasn't returned?"

"I'm sorry," Oberon said gently.

Gwen couldn't stand it another second. "Who?" she asked, striding into the grove. "Who hasn't come back?"

"Gwen!" Devin gave a whoop of joy, then lifted her up and spun her in a gleeful circle. "You're all right!"

"Yes, I'm fine!" Gwen said, laughing. She waited until Devin set her down to explain that Titania had healed her.

"Thank goodness for that!" Devin was looking at her as though she were some sort of miracle.

Gwen was finding it hard to sort out her own emotions. She was so glad to see her twin safe, so grateful for all he'd done, she didn't even know where to start.

"Devin," she said at last, "I want to thank you for rescuing me and Thomas, and to tell you how positively brilliant you were, and how that poet's shirt you wore was really a great improvement over your usual wardrobe, but—can all that wait for later? I'm just so glad to see you!" With that, she threw her arms around her brother and hugged him.

"I suppose I get no thanks at all!" the pooka said indignantly.

Gwen wiped a tear from her eye. "You were the one who carried me back, weren't you?"

"You *and* the Rhymer!" the pooka said. "Really, you'd think I were a transport service."

"I'd never have made it without you," Gwen said. "Please accept my deepest thanks."

Pooka flashed her a gleaming white smile. "I hear you can do a very flattering likeness. I'll take a portrait, if you don't mind."

Gwen curtsied to him. "It will be my pleasure." She turned to Oberon, suddenly aware that she'd been ignoring the King of Faery, and dropped him a deeper curtsy. "I hope you'll excuse me," she said hurriedly. "I'm Gwenevere and—"

"I know who you are, child, and I think we can dispense with formalities," Oberon told her.

"I'll leave you and your brother for now. Pooka, come along and give them some peace."

Devin smiled happily at his sister. "I missed you, you know."

"I missed you, too," Gwen said. "Terribly. But Dev, who were you talking about before with Oberon? Was there someone who went to the Raven Queen's hall and didn't come back?"

The happy expression left Devin's face. "She was a faery...when she wasn't a weasel, that is. Her name was Weasel Faery, and she helped me, and then, just when Pooka tied me up, she disappeared. She reminded me of that little rodent in your tapestry. She had the most extraordinary green eyes."

"The mink!" Gwen gasped.

"What?"

"I think I know where she is, and it's not in Nicnevin's court. But she's been...changed," Gwen added. "We'll need Titania's magic to restore her to her true form."

Gwen led her brother to the mink footstool. "Is this your faery?"

"Weasel!" cried the boy. He picked up the footstool and cradled it tenderly in his arms. They started toward the ruined palace, and Devin gave his sister a curious look. "How did you know to bring her out from under the hill?"

"I didn't," Gwen admitted. "I had no idea she

was a faery or that she had helped you. I just saw Nicnevin turn her into a footstool, and I couldn't bear to leave her there a prisoner. Don't worry. I'm sure Titania can help her own faery."

As the twins approached Titania with the footstool, Thomas rose to greet them. "I owe you both my deepest thanks," the Rhymer said. "For my life."

Gwen blushed and Dev grinned. "I had some help," he explained, touching the ring that Titania had given him.

"Indeed," Thomas said. "But there was more than the Seelie Court's magic at work when you won our freedom. You were well named, lad."

Gwen's eyebrows rose. "What do you mean?"

"Devin." Thomas told her. "It's an old Gaelic name that means poet or bard."

Now it was Devin's turn to blush and he quickly changed the subject, holding the footstool out to the Faery Queen. "This is Weasel," he told her. "She went under the hill to try to help us and Nicnevin changed her into a footstool. Won't you please change her back?"

Titania shook her head sadly. "I'm sorry," she said. "This is not within my power."

"It has to be!" Gwen said, and instantly regretted her words. When would she ever learn not to argue with faery queens?

The hint of a smile played at the edges of Titania's mouth. "Actually, Gwenevere, if Weasel is to be restored to her true form, it is you who must do it."

"Me?" Gwen stared at the Queen of Faery, wondering if she were being mocked. "But I don't know anything about magic."

"Don't you?" Titania asked.

Gwen looked desperately at Devin, who handed her the footstool, then raised his shoulders in an eloquent shrug.

Gwen petted the wooden animal, feeling helpless. "I—I call on the magic of this forest and ask you to return to your true form!" she tried.

The footstool remained as it was.

She tried again. "I *command* you to return to your true form." Still a footstool. Gwen gave Titania an imploring look. "I don't know any words of power," she explained.

Titania's eyes were cool. "You don't need them. Your power is not in words, child."

"Oh, for pity's sake!" The cry of exasperation came from the Rhymer. "Must you immortals always speak in riddles?" He stepped toward Gwen and gave her the same reassuring look he'd given her in Nicnevin's throne room. "You've done this before, Gwen," he said softly.

Gwen blinked in disbelief. "I have?"

Thomas leaned forward, holding open his

pocket. The little mouse with the bent whisker appeared, its pink nose eagerly sniffing.

"B-but that was the magic of the Raven Queen's realm," Gwen protested.

Thomas shot a questioning look at Titania.

"Tell her," the Faery Queen agreed.

"Your power is in your art, Gwenevere. You have the power to create, which carries as much magic as any faery spell. Your work when done with love gives life to things—in our world, to art. And in this world, where things are a little different, your art can give life to those who've had it drained from them."

"Oh," Gwenevere said. She hardly dared believe the Rhymer's words, and yet... "Could I have a charcoal pencil, please, and a sheet of paper?" she asked.

Oberon clapped his hands, and a small faery wearing a tiny painter's smock brought paper and charcoal.

Gwen fixed the mink with her "bird eye" and began to draw. She could feel her hands trembling. She had to do this right. She couldn't risk bringing a mink with misshapen ears or backward whiskers to life. This drawing had to be perfect. She rubbed out a tense, awkward line and drew it again, this time loose and flowing, following the line of the mink's back. She sketched in the face and the delicate paws, and though she didn't have a green pencil, she drew bright life and keen intelligence in the eyes.

She was perfecting the fur when Dev cried, "You've done it!"

Gwen snapped out of her trance and saw that her subject was no longer a footstool. The little animal's whiskers were twitching, her sides rising and falling with gentle breaths. She looked about, then scurried directly to Devin and climbed his pants and shirt, coming to rest with her nose nestled against his neck.

"It's you!" he said happily.

"It's me," Weasel replied.

Gwen stared at her own charcoal-smudged hand in amazement. "I did it," she breathed. "I brought the mink back to life!"

"I'm not a mink, I'm a weasel!" the little creature snapped. "Get it right—a weasel!"

Gwen grinned. "No, you're a faery. Only a faery would be brought back to life and scold me straight off."

The pooka placed himself directly between Gwen and Devin, giving the little faery a disdainful glance. "You've spent enough time on Weasel," he declared. "Now you must draw me, and that shall require three drawings."

"Three?" Gwen echoed, puzzled.

In the blink of an eye, the pooka shifted from

goat-man to black dog to white horse, then back to goat-man again. "Of course," he said. "One drawing for each of my fascinating forms."

Dawn was breaking, and the sky was a pale blue tinged with coral. The twins stood on the bow of the *Basset,* the wind whipping their hair back from their faces. The ship had come for them the night before, just as Gwen finished her third drawing of the pooka, necessitating quick farewells to Titania, Oberon, Thomas, and the pooka. Weasel Faery, being a Cornish faery, had decided to return home with them.

Gwen was glad to be back aboard the *Basset.* She and Devin had had a lovely reunion with the dwarves and gremlins, and though Weasel claimed to be a bit seasick, they'd had calm seas and a smooth journey. Now the port of St. Ives was in sight. Gwen could even make out the white houses of Pembrook Crescent.

"I can't believe we're almost home," she said to her brother. "It seems like we set sail from the island barely an hour ago."

"Time seems to do funny things in the realm of the imagination," Devin observed. He stroked Weasel, who was peeking out of the pack that hung from his shoulder. "Still, it's a good thing we're almost there. We've been away longer than I ever expected. Mama and Papa must be out of their heads with worry by now."

Gwen winced. "Do you think they've notified the constable?"

"Scotland Yard," Dev joked, twisting the ring that Titania had given him. "No, the Aisling sisters must have told them where you went. And, hopefully, someone in that house will be sensible enough to figure out that I went with you."

"Who? The parrot?"

Devin laughed. "You've got a point. Being sensible isn't exactly our strong suit at Camelot."

"It's yours," Gwen said, "and I can't tell you how badly I missed it when I was in the Raven Queen's hall."

The boy gave her a small smile, but his eyes were locked on the port ahead of them.

"What's wrong?" Gwen asked. "Are you sorry we're going home? Are you missing the Realm?"

"Not when I've got Weasel with me," Devin answered. Weasel licked his hand appreciatively. "It's just that...for a little while there, I knew what it felt like to be a musician, performing in a royal court. And I got to be a bit of a hero when I rescued you. And now I'm going home—to be the sensible one!"

Gwen thought about that. "Well, you *are* the sensible one," she admitted, adjusting her blue velvet cape. "And it's a good thing, because we'd all fall apart without you—just look at how much trouble *I* got in! But you're more than that, Dev."

"I know. I'm practical. And responsible," he added with a sigh.

"No." Gwen tugged on her brother's shoulder until he looked at her. "You're an artist, too, only your art is in words. You're a storyteller, like Thomas."

"No, I'm not. That was Oberon's spell. He gave me the power to play the harp and sing. But only to rescue you. I can't do it anymore."

"I'm *not* talking about your singing," Gwen said. "I'm talking about that incredible story you told. It was as beautiful as any painting. It had power. It was magic. You *are* an artist, Dev, and your art set us free."

"I don't think so," Devin said sadly.

Gwen bit her lip. She wasn't sure how to convince her brother of what she was saying, but she knew that convincing him was important. She sensed that this mattered very deeply to Devin, and if he returned home believing he had no talent—only to be surrounded by people congratulating him for being sensible—then he might close his heart to the truth.

She looked up at the *Basset*'s banner for inspiration, then said, "Don't you remember what Nicnevin told you? She said she'd never heard a finer story since Taliesin's time."

"Nicnevin!" Devin spat. "She's a trustworthy one!"

"She *is*," Gwen said. "When I was under the hill, one of the fairies there—one whom I couldn't stand—told me that faeries are different from us because they can't lie. It goes against their magic somehow. And I thought about it, and I thought of all the horrid things this particular faery had said to me, and Nicnevin, as well, and I realized that there wasn't a lie in any of it."

Dev gave his sister a sideways glance. "I thought Nicnevin told you that you had no talent."

Gwen winced. The memory still stung. "She did. But I think from her point of view it was true. What can I say? She's got a good ear for music and stories, but no eye for drawings at all!"

Devin grinned and put a hand on her shoulder. "Look, I appreciate you trying to make me feel better, but—"

Gwen cut him off. "There's something else Nicnevin told me. She said that the Realm reveals your true nature. And she was right. It revealed you to be not only practical and sensible but smart and courageous and an amazing storyteller. Dev, if you don't believe me and you stop spinning those incredible stories, then we'll all have lost something rich and beautiful."

Gwen saw a gleam of hope in her brother's

eyes. "Are you absolutely sure?" he asked.

"Absolutely positive," she replied, tossing back her hair.

"Port of St. Ives!" Sebastian called out a short time later. "All ashore that's going ashore!"

Gwen watched with amusement as the gremlins lifted her valise and toted it to the gangplank. Devin was shaking hands with Sebastian and Archimedes and taking one last look at the *wuntarlabe*.

"Now, don't try to tell your family about your adventures on the faery island," Sebastian was advising. "Families aren't capable of understanding or believing such things."

Devin grinned. "You haven't met our family. Believing in faeries is their specialty. What they *won't* be able to understand is why I'm so interested in a device like the *wuntarlabe*."

Gwen walked up to Captain Malachi and said, "Thank you. I appreciate all the help you gave us. Especially the gremlins' sewing the painting into my dress."

The captain tipped his hat to her. "It was our pleasure, Miss Gwenevere. Anything for a friend of the Aislings." He peered over the side of the ship and a smile lit his face. "And there they are now!"

Indeed, the Aislings were standing on the

dock along with Mrs. Thornworth. "Mama!" Gwen cried, waving madly, and was very glad to see her mother wave back.

The instant the gremlins lowered the gangplank, Gwen raced down it and into her mother's arms.

"Hullo, princess," May Thornworth said. "Are you all right?" She opened her arms for Devin, too. "And you, my wonderful, practical boy. Are you both quite all right?"

"We're fine, Mama," Gwen assured her. "You weren't terribly worried, were you?"

May Thornworth nodded toward the Aisling sisters, who were greeting the *Basset*'s crew. "The Aislings told me that you were delivering my portrait, and when I couldn't find Devin... Actually, it was Cook who suggested he might have gone with you. Did the painting get to Professor Aisling?"

"We hear he was delighted with it," Gwen reported proudly. "But, Mama—what did Papa say? Was he worried about us?"

"I don't think your father even noticed you were gone," their mother confessed. "He's been up all night in the studio, getting ready for the big London exhibition."

Something in her tone made Devin ask, "How long do you think we've been gone, then?"

"Since last night, of course," Mrs. Thornworth replied. "But the Aislings assured me you'd be back in time for breakfast. And it's a good thing. That blasted parrot escaped its cage again and is flying madly about the house. Cook is making griddle cakes, and your sisters are back with a young photographer from London. He photographs faeries. Apparently, the prints are quite authentic."

The twins exchanged a glance. Things were perfectly normal at Camelot.

Mrs. Thornworth quickly drew back the arm she had around her son, a look of alarm on her face.

"Devin," she said, "what's that furry thing crawling out of your pack?" She peered more closely. "Why, it looks like that little creature in the tapestry. My goodness—it *is* a ferret!"

"It's a *weasel!*" said Gwen and Devin together.

"Are you sure it's a weasel and not a ferret?" their mother asked.

Weasel stood up on her hind legs, extended a delicate paw to Mrs. Thornworth, and said, "Absolutely positive!"

A Note from the Authors

We'd like to thank James C. Christensen, who created the *Basset;* our editor, Jim Thomas, who invited us on board; and Tanith Lee, who journeyed into the Lands of Legend before us.

Readers might like to know that the faeries in this book (both the Seelie and Unseelie Courts, and the Dark Queen Nicnevin) come from the old folktales of the British Isles. You can spell "faery" many different ways: fairy, feary, fayry... but however you spell it, don't say it out loud unless you want to call the faeries' attention!

If you'd like to learn more about faeries, we recommend *An Encyclopedia of Fairies* and *British Folktales* by Katherine Briggs and *Fairy Mythology* by Thomas Keightley, as well as the following two books of faery art: *Faeries* by Alan Lee and Brian Froud, and *Good Faeries, Bad Faeries,* by Brian Froud. There are even two good faery Web sites: "Faeries," at faeryland.tamu-commerce.edu/~earendil/faerie/index.html, and "The World of Froud," at www.faeries.net.

Like King Arthur, Thomas the Rhymer is a figure found in both folklore and history. He's best known as the hero of a Middle English ballad about a minstrel named Thomas, who is taken by the Queen of Elfland to her realm for seven years. It's said that when he left Faery, he could speak only the truth and was given the gift of prophecy. This is why he is believed to be Thomas of Erceldoune, who lived in Scotland in the thirteenth century and was a famous poet and prophet. If you go to the little town of Earlston, Scotland (which is southeast of Edinburgh), you can stop at the modern Rhymer's Tower Café and see the ruins of Thomas's Tower out back! The story of Thomas the Rhymer was recently retold by Sharyn McCrumb in the Green Man Press comic book *Ballads, Volume 1,* illustrated by Charles Vess. You can also find the original poem there.

Although Gwen and Devin's parents, John and May Thornworth, were not real people, there *was* a group of artists in England about a hundred years ago known as the Pre-Raphaelites. Dante Gabriel Rossetti, John Millais, Edward Burne-Jones, and William Morris (all mentioned in the first chapter of this book) were real people. They loved to paint King Arthur and fairy-tale scenes, and were just as eccentric as the Thornworths. *The Pre-Raphaelites* by Christopher Wood and *Pre-Raphaelite Women* by Jan Marsh are two books filled with beautiful examples of Pre-Raphaelite art. There are also two good Pre-Raphaelite Web sites: "Webmagick," at www.webmagick.co.uk, and "The Germ," at www.walrus.com/~gibralto/acorn/germ.

Thanks for sailing with us!
Terri Windling and
Ellen Steiber

ABOUT THE AUTHORS

TERRI WINDLING (who wrote the Devin chapters in this book) has loved magical tales ever since she was a small girl. She always wanted to live in an old stone cottage like the ones in fairy-tale illustrations—and now she does, in the west of England (not far from Cornwall), every summer. In the winter, she lives in the Arizona desert. She is the author of two other books for children, *A Midsummer Night's Faery Tale* and *The Changeling*. She created the *Borderland* series for teenage readers and won the Mythopoeic Award for her adult novel *The Wood Wife*. She has also won five World Fantasy Awards. You can visit her Web site at www.endicott-studio.com.

ELLEN STEIBER (who wrote the Gwenevere chapters) was given a book of fairy tales by her aunt Dolly when she was six and has been in love with folklore and stories of magic ever since. She's now written over twenty-five books for young readers (many of them series fiction) as well as fantasy short stories and novellas for adults and teens, and has won a Golden Kite Award. Her work has been published in the *Snow White, Blood Red* series; *The Armless Maiden; The Magazine of Fantasy & Science Fiction;* and other venues. She lives in Arizona with Terri Windling, two cats, and lots of coyotes.